A heart-wrenching cry sounded from behind her.

At the top of the steps, right outside the door, was a large white wicker basket with a white blanket spilling out of it. Next to that was a pink vinyl bag. Everything clicked together in her mind. The cries, the basket, that pink bag. No. *No, no, no.* Please. No one could be that cruel, that heartless, that... irresponsible. Could they?

Emma sprinted for the steps, her pulse rushing in her ears as she dropped to her knees beside the basket. She flipped back the white blanket. The crying stopped. But that's when Emma's tears started and tracked down her face. She yanked out her phone and dialed 911 just as she noticed the short cryptic note taped to the basket's handle.

Please take care of my angel.

This book is dedicated to my agent, Nalini Akolekar, and my Harlequin Intrigue editors, Allison Lyons and Denise Zaza, for their patience and support when I faced some tough family and health problems while writing this book. Your kindness and understanding mean *everything* to me. Thank you.

POLICE DOG PROCEDURAL

LENA DIAZ

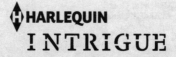

HARLEQUIN
INTRIGUE

Special thanks and acknowledgment are given to Lena Diaz for her contribution to the K-9s on Patrol miniseries.

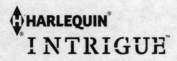

Recycling programs for this product may not exist in your area.

ISBN-13: 978-1-335-58223-2

Police Dog Procedural

Harlequin Enterprises ULC
22 Adelaide St. West, 41st Floor
Toronto, Ontario M5H 4E3, Canada
www.Harlequin.com

Printed in U.S.A.

Lena Diaz was born in Kentucky and has also lived in California, Louisiana and Florida, where she now resides with her husband and two children. Before becoming a romantic suspense author, she was a computer programmer. A Romance Writers of America Golden Heart® Award finalist, she has also won the prestigious Daphne du Maurier Award for Excellence in Mystery/Suspense. To get the latest news about Lena, please visit her website, lenadiaz.com.

Books by Lena Diaz

Harlequin Intrigue

Police Dog Procedural

A Tennessee Cold Case Story

Murder on Prescott Mountain
Serial Slayer Cold Case

The Justice Seekers

Cowboy Under Fire
Agent Under Siege
Killer Conspiracy
Deadly Double-Cross

The Mighty McKenzies

Smoky Mountains Ranger
Smokies Special Agent
Conflicting Evidence
Undercover Rebel

Tennessee SWAT

Mountain Witness
Secret Stalker
Stranded with the Detective
SWAT Standoff

Visit the Author Profile page at Harlequin.com.

CAST OF CHARACTERS

Lieutenant Macon Ridley—Macon and his K-9 partner give up their violent Boise, Idaho, taskforce jobs to work in the quiet mountain town of Jaspar. But violence seems to have followed them.

Emma Daniels—Emma escaped an abusive childhood and found peace training K-9s and their humans at the Daniels Canine Academy (DCA). But when trouble comes calling, she must learn to open her heart to Macon and trust him, or they'll both pay the price.

Hugh Engel—This troubled teen is doing court-ordered volunteer work at DCA. Is he taking out his resentment by causing trouble for Emma?

William Shrader—Hugh's sidekick seems unlikely to be involved in the recent spate of crimes. But maybe he's hiding a dark side.

Kyle Norvell—Where Kyle leads, Hugh and William follow. Macon is determined to stop him before he leads his friends straight to prison or someone gets killed.

Captain Arthur Rutledge—With the looks of a movie star and the scruples of a rattlesnake, Rutledge makes no secret that once he's promoted to chief, he'll suspend the K-9 partnership with DCA. But is he trying to ruin DCA to ensure his promotion doesn't slip away?

Chapter One

The painful echoes of the past whipped through Emma's mind, chilling her far more than the autumn winds funneling down from Idaho's Salmon River Mountains. She perched on the top step of her covered back deck, clutching a steaming coffee cup in her hands. The predawn sky began to lighten to a soft gray, allowing a first glimpse of the rolling land around her. But it wasn't the K-9 training ring that she saw. Or the small horse paddock encircled by a white three-rail fence. Or even the golden larch trees just beginning to turn yellow amid the deep greens of the Douglas firs and western white pines. What she saw didn't exist, not anymore. And yet it was as brutally real this morning as it had been when she was a little girl.

Maybe it was the surprisingly crisp chill of this late-September morning that had triggered the memories she usually managed to keep locked away. It had been an unseasonably cool day much like this one when she'd last seen her biological parents. Her fa-

ther had been using her as a punching bag—again—
while her mother sat on the other side of the room in
a drunken stupor, ignoring Emma's cries for help.
She'd ignored Danny's and Katie's cries, too.

Emma had been the lucky one. She wasn't hurt
so badly that she couldn't go to school. And her father hadn't been careful enough about where he'd hit
her this time. When her second-grade teacher caught
sight of suspicious-looking bruises peeking out from
beneath Emma's long sleeves, she'd called the Jasper
police. DCF, the Department of Child and Family
Services, had taken Emma away. But they were too
late to help her sister and brother.

Emma's hands tightened around her coffee mug as
the dark memories swirled. After being released from
the hospital, she'd been placed with foster parents,
K-9 unit Officer Rick Daniels and his community-
minded wife, Susan. If not for them, and the teacher
who'd refused to ignore the signs that others had,
Emma would have been sleeping with the angels by
now. Just like Danny and Katie.

Swallowing past the tightness in her throat, she
sent up a prayer of thanks that she, at least, was
spared. And that her birth parents were both in prison
where they could never hurt another child. Twenty-
three years. Had it really been that long since that
awful day when she'd lost her siblings?

Another chilly breeze had her taking a deep sip of
the hot coffee. She reveled in the burn that warmed
her insides—much as Rick and Susan's patient love

and understanding had warmed her heart. Somehow, they'd eventually thawed out the ice around it that had enabled her to survive the eight long years of beatings, hunger and neglect. She thought about them, and missed them, every day. But it was the loss of her police officer father that hurt the most. Because he was the one who'd taught by example and helped her learn to trust again. He'd taught her that not all men were bad. He'd shown her that a real man, even if he was big and strong, used his strength to help others, not hurt them.

But even big, strong Rick Daniels wasn't impervious to a bullet.

When Officer Walters had broken the news that Rick and Duke, his K-9 partner, weren't ever coming home again, it had sent Emma into a dangerous tailspin. It had taken years for her to emerge from that dark place. And yet another police officer, like her dad, to help pull her out of it. Walters had done everything he could to turn her away from the destructive path she'd gone down. Thanks to him, and her dear mother, Susan, Emma had finally put her demons behind her.

Thank God the cancer had waited to take her mother until after Emma had straightened out. Susan had lived long enough to see Emma go to college. They'd made some wonderful memories that helped tide Emma over whenever grief reared its ugly head. Or when the other thoughts came, the ugly ones from her childhood.

She squeezed her eyes shut, wishing she could close her ears just as easily. The screams from her past were louder than ever, making her cringe against the sound of fear that had once been her constant companion.

Another scream tore through the air as the sun's first rays warmed her face. Her eyes flew open. Those weren't the sounds of her past. This was happening right now. Someone else was on the ranch, and they were crying, desperate for help.

She jumped to her feet, cursing when hot coffee sloshed onto her hand. She tossed the cup on the ground. The dogs were barking now, probably had been for a while. She'd been so caught up in her thoughts that she hadn't noticed. Something was wrong, horribly wrong. And that mournful sound was coming from the *front* of the property.

She took off running, her boots digging into the grass and gravel as she whipped around the side of the house. Belatedly, she realized she should have gone inside and grabbed a gun first. No telling what she was about to find. But she couldn't ignore those anguished cries for even one more second. She rounded the corner and skidded to a halt in the gravel out front.

No one was there.

The cries had stopped.

The dogs were no longer barking.

She looked past the circular drive, past the wishing well in the middle, toward the arched entry to the ranch a good hundred yards west. Both her property manager and head trainer would be here soon. But their usual parking spaces to the left of the kennels just past the circular drive were empty except for Emma's rusty pickup truck. The only other vehicle was Shane's RV, backed into its usual spot between the kennels and the small barn that housed her two horses. All was silent. Everything looked as it should, and yet something seemed...off.

Was someone hiding just inside the clumps of evergreens on the far side of the clearing, watching her?

Or hunkered down behind the wishing well a few yards away?

Did they know about her past and make those awful cries, realizing she'd feel compelled to run out here to help?

She cautiously backed toward the porch steps behind her as she continued to scan the trees, hills and outbuildings. Unfortunately, trouble was no stranger here at the Daniels Canine Academy. Part of it had been Emma's fault, during her rebellious period after her father's death when she'd hooked up with a bad boy, Billy. But later, as an adult, she'd brought even more problems to the ranch when she'd fostered troubled youths. The Jasper police had already been familiar with DCA because Emma trained their K-9s. But they'd become even more familiar because of her calls for assistance on numerous occasions. But that was years ago. She hadn't fostered anyone for quite some time.

But she did have three at-risk high-school boys working part time here at DCA on weekends as part of their court-ordered community service.

William Shrader, Hugh Engel, and Kyle Norvell were a tight-knit group of friends. Emma had met with their families several times since the boys began working here to report on their progress. The parents all seemed nice enough and genuinely concerned about their sons. And the boys hadn't given her any trouble. But for only being in high school, they each had a shockingly long history of trouble with the law.

She slowed to a halt, hating where her mind was going. She didn't want to believe the worst. But experience told her she couldn't ignore the obvious— that the boys were forced by a judge to work here as part of an agreement to stay out of jail. They hadn't been working here for very long. Their resentment toward the judge could easily transfer to Emma. And she hadn't known them long enough to establish any real trust between them. She had no idea what they might be capable of.

If one of them was behind the screams, it could be a prank. It could also be something more sinister, dangerous. She *really* wished she'd gone inside for a gun.

She cautiously backed a few more steps toward the covered porch that ran across the front of the little one-story house. A heart-wrenching cry sounded behind her. She whirled around. At the top of the steps, right outside the door, was a large wicker basket with a white blanket spilling out of it. Next to that was a pink vinyl bag.

Everything clicked together in her mind. The cries, the basket, that pink bag. No. *No, no, no.* Please. No one could be that cruel, that heartless, that…irresponsible, especially as cold as it was out here this morning. Could they? Well of course they could. She knew better than most that people could be cruel, heartless and downright *mean.*

She sprinted forward and fairly flew up the steps. Her pulse rushed in her ears as she dropped to her knees beside the basket and then flipped back the white blanket. The crying stopped. Tears spilled down Emma's cheeks as she yanked her cell phone out of her jacket pocket and dialed 911.

A chill wind ruffled her hair and made a piece of paper flutter where it had been taped to the top of the basket handle. It was a cryptic note.

Please take care of my Angel.

"Jasper police, what's your emergency?" a familiar-sounding young woman's voice asked through the phone.

"Jenny, it's Emma Daniels, at DCA. Someone trespassed on my property and—"

"Are you okay, Emma? Are they still at your ranch?"

"No, I mean, yes, I'm home. And yes, I'm fine. No one's here. At least, I don't think so, except—"

"I'm dispatching some deputies right now. I can send an ambulance, too, just to be sure you're okay. It's no trouble."

An ambulance? Did she need one? It was chilly, but not freezing. And the temps would soar into the seventies as the sun rose higher. How long had the baby been left outside?

Dread had her heart lurching in her chest. She looked down again, then smiled through her tears as she lifted the precious bundle. "I don't think we need an ambulance. But, yes, please, send one. Just to be sure. I really think she's okay."

"Who's okay? Emma? Who's there with you?"

"Someone sneaked onto the ranch and left something by my front door—"

"What did they leave?"

She hugged the bundle closer and tugged her jacket around it, rocking back and forth as she looked into the baby's dark brown eyes. "An angel. They left me an angel."

Chapter Two

Lieutenant Macon Ridley slowed his Dodge Durango just enough to make the turn off South Elm onto 1 Daniels Way without fishtailing. As soon as he passed beneath the Daniels Canine Academy archway with its silhouette of a German shepherd, he gunned the engine. Dirt and gravel kicked up from his tires, spitting across the grass and pinging off nearby trees as he rushed up the long driveway. He didn't slow until he was a few car lengths from the modest, white-washed brick ranch house with its familiar green roof. He yanked the wheel, pulling the SUV to a rocking halt just short of the porch steps.

He was out in a flash, right hand resting on his holster as he scanned his surroundings. Off to the left, a concrete-and-wood building housed the dozen or so dog kennels as well as an office. There was an RV parked to the right of the kennels. That was new since he'd last been here. Next to the RV was a small white barn that he knew served as a home for Emma's two rescue horses. Past that, even though he couldn't

see it, was a fenced-in area that he remembered doubled as an agility training arena for the K-9s and a
paddock for the horses.

Everything seemed neat, orderly, pristine, which
fit right in with his memories of Emma. But the place
was quiet. Too quiet for a place where a 911 call had
been placed just minutes earlier. Where was she? In
the house? Alone? He didn't have much to go on from
what dispatch had said. Just that some trespassers
had allegedly left their surprise—a baby—on her
porch and taken off. But they could have been hiding, waiting until Emma got off the phone. Jenny
had tried to keep Emma on the line, per policy, but
she'd insisted she was fine and needed to focus on
caring for the infant. Macon had no way of knowing
whether something else had happened after she hung
up. She could be in trouble right now. And the decisions he made in the next few minutes were critical.

Please let her be okay.

A whimper sounded from the back seat. His black
shepherd pressed his nose against the window, just
as anxious as Macon to find out what was going on.

"Easy, Bogie." He yanked open the door and
quickly attached the leash to the K-9's collar.

Bogie hopped out and Macon gave an instruc-
tion in German, adding the shepherd's more formal
name at the end, Bogart. That had the dog's ears
perking up. He was all business now, muscles taut
as he strained on the leash, his gaze riveted on the

house. Macon tightened his grip and together they bounded up the porch steps.

He drew his gun, holding it down by his right side while keeping a tight hold on Bogie's leash with his left hand.

"Police!" He shoved open the door without waiting for an answer and hurried inside.

He and Bogie were halfway across the main living area when a wide-eyed Emma rushed out of the kitchen opening at the back left corner of the house.

Cradling a baby against her chest.

If Jenny hadn't warned him, he'd have been surprised and confused to see Emma holding an infant. Judging by the shocked look on Emma's face, Jenny hadn't bothered to warn her about him. She definitely hadn't expected Macon to be the one who'd respond to her 911 call. Unfortunately, he didn't have time to explain.

He quickly scanned the room, making sure no one was hiding anywhere and paying special attention to his K-9 partner. Bogie was alert, but not giving an indication that he sensed anyone else aside from Emma…and the baby.

Macon strode forward and gently pushed Emma back so he and Bogie could make a quick sweep of the kitchen. After checking the walk-in pantry, he made sure the back door was locked, with the dead bolt engaged. Turning around, he moved past Emma again.

"Anyone else inside?" he called out as he and Bogie

headed toward the hallway that opened off the back of the living room.

"No. No, it's just me. And Angel." Her voice wobbled, sounding strained, which wasn't characteristic of strong, confident Emma.

Keeping a watchful eye on the doors down the hallway, he gave Bogie another order in German. They quickly cleared the three small bedrooms, lone bathroom, and handful of closets before returning to the main room.

Emma was standing by the front door, which was now closed and dead-bolted.

He nodded his approval and holstered his gun. A quick command to Bogie had him sitting on the floor beside him. Gone was the tense, all-business K-9 ready to sacrifice himself to protect others. In his place was a hundred-pound teddy bear with his pink tongue lolling out, his adoring gaze fixed on Emma. Obviously Bogie hadn't forgotten her over the past two years any more than Macon had. And as she glanced from the dog to him, it was obvious that she hadn't forgotten them either.

Her brow knit with confusion as she clutched the bundle against her chest. "Macon? I don't understand. Did you come back here for more training and Jenny asked you to check on..." She seemed to suddenly take in his black uniform and the shield on his shoulder depicting the mountains and an eagle eyeing a salmon in the river. "That's a *Jasper PD* uniform. You're not with the canine task force in Boise anymore?"

Before he could answer, the dual sound of a siren out front and his radio squawking on his shoulder went off.

Emma turned toward the window. An ambulance was idling just past the archway at the end of the long drive. Lights flashed, but the siren was off now.

Macon reported in, letting Jenny know that the house was clear but to keep holding the ambulance at the entrance until he cleared the rest of the property.

"Emma, I need to check the outbuildings, make sure no one is hiding anywhere outside before the ambulance can come up here. Unless there's an urgency for medical attention for you, or the baby. If that's the case, I'll drive you both to the entrance—"

"No, no." She tightened her hold, shifting the bundle higher. "She seems fine. We'll wait. I didn't see anyone out there. I'm guessing they took off after they left Angel."

"The baby's name is Angel?"

She shrugged. "I'm not sure. But the note made it sound that way." She motioned toward a basket sitting off to the side with a piece of paper taped to the handle.

He wanted to read it, take the paper and the basket into evidence. But he couldn't yet. First, he had to make sure Emma and the baby were safe. "That RV outside, is anyone—"

"No, no. It's empty. Shane keeps it here because there isn't any room to park it at his and Piper's place."

He nodded even though he had no clue who Shane

was. Piper, he remembered, was a friend of Emma's who worked at DCA. "Flip the dead bolt behind me."

"Will do." She put her hand on his arm as he unlocked the door to leave. "Thanks, Macon. I don't know what's going on, why you're wearing a Jasper uniform, but it's good to see you. And with you and Bogie here, I know we're safe."

Her face pinkened with a light blush as if she regretted the uncharacteristic spilling of emotion.

He gave her a reassuring look, wishing he didn't have to leave her even for a few minutes. He'd never seen fear in her eyes until now. And it bothered him far more than he'd have expected.

"We'll be right back." After a quick command to *Bogart*, they were out the door, the shepherd once again on full alert.

It didn't take long to inspect the kennels and small barn and verify that the storage sheds on the property were locked tight. The RV was locked, too, and there were no signs that anyone had broken in. The lack of fresh footprints in the dirt beside the RV and Bogie's disinterest in it made him confident that no one was hiding inside.

The sound of a siren had him pausing by some bushes near the porch. Another Jasper PD SUV whipped past the idling ambulance and sped up the driveway. The backup that Jenny had promised had arrived. And as they neared, he realized it was Lieutenant Cal Hoover and rookie officer Jason Wright. Macon signaled, letting them know all was clear.

"Come on, boy." He tugged on Bogie's leash so they could greet the other officers. A whine had him turning to see why the dog wasn't following.

Bogie wasn't trained as a scent dog. He couldn't sniff out bombs or drugs, or track a lost child. He was trained for suspect apprehension and attack. But he had great instincts and had definitely smelled something he didn't like. He whined again, sniffing the air and pushing his body between Macon and the bushes.

Macon whipped his pistol out and trained it on the overgrown shrubs. Moments later, the two cops who'd just pulled up were shoulder to shoulder with him, their pistols also trained on the thick greenery where someone could easily hide. But it only took a few seconds for the three of them, along with the dog, to verify no one was there.

He exchanged a perplexed look with his brothers in blue and was just about to force Bogie away from the greenery when he realized what was bothering the shepherd. One of the lower branches on the bush closest to the edge of the porch was broken. And impaled on the sharp end was a small piece of white cloth that looked suspiciously similar to the blanket Emma had wrapped around the baby. Had the person who'd abandoned the baby hidden here and caught the blanket on the bush? If so, then the baby, and torn piece of blanket, weren't all they'd left.

They'd also left a smear of blood.

Chapter Three

Emma leaned to the side, trying to see past the two EMTs who were examining Angel on top of the kitchen table. "It can't be Angel's blood on those bushes. I checked her all over to make sure she was okay. There weren't any cuts."

The larger of the two men glanced up at her but didn't say anything as the other man pulled open the diaper.

Emma went rigid with fear as the reason for that part of the examination swept through her. "No," she whispered, pressing her hand to her mouth. "No. Please, God. Anything but that."

Suddenly Macon was beside her, his shoulder pressed to hers in a show of support. She clenched her hands together, waiting silently along with the two other officers—Cal Hoover and Jason Wright—who were squeezed into her tiny kitchen.

The first EMT re-taped the diaper into place and smiled at Emma. "A doctor will check her again, but

I don't see any signs of trauma. I'm guessing she's a couple of months old, if that. Seems healthy."

Relief had her slumping against Macon. He stood strong and steady, giving her support in more ways than one. She smiled her thanks, then watched as Angel was bundled up again. The EMT who'd been examining the baby hurried out of the kitchen and strode toward the front door while the other one quickly repacked the box of supplies they'd brought inside.

"I want to ride along with her to the hospital," Emma said. "Just let me grab my purse."

"Not enough room," the EMT told her. "And the county insurance doesn't allow anyone else to ride back there."

"You won't even know I'm there," she insisted. "I'll stay out of your way. And I won't tell anyone."

He arched a brow and glanced at the three policemen in the room, then shook his head and snapped the box shut. "Sorry, but no."

"Get your purse, Emma." Macon's deep voice snapped her attention back to him instead of the second EMT who was now moving toward the front door.

She nodded, confident Macon would handle the situation, and hurried to her bedroom to grab her purse and phone. But when she got back to the living room, the house was empty. A quick glance out the front windows showed the ambulance speeding down the driveway away from the house.

She swore and rushed onto the porch just as Bogie hopped into the back of Macon's SUV. Macon shut the door and turned to face her as she hurried down the steps.

"Why did they leave without me?" she demanded. "I want to be there for Angel."

"And you will be. Just not in the ambulance. There really wasn't room back there and they wouldn't let you inside the emergency room with her anyway. Plus, you'll need a ride home from the hospital later. I figured I'd offer my services. We can sit in the waiting room together until the doctor finishes his exam. And I can take your official statement while we wait so you don't have to go to the station." He strode to the passenger side and opened the door, motioning behind her. "Cal and Jason will stay here to collect the blood evidence and search for other clues about who left the baby. They can lock up when they're done. I saw you had extra keys hanging by the front door. We'll talk about a safer place to keep them later. I assume one of them is a house key?"

She rolled her eyes and nodded, then turned to see Cal directing Jason, the rookie who was once a troubled teen she'd fostered here at DCA. She couldn't help smiling, remembering how good he'd been with the horses in particular. He'd absolutely adored her quarter horse, Presley. But what was even more rewarding was having watched him a few months earlier when he and a young woman she'd also fostered as a teen, Tashya, got married. But her smile faded in light of what Jason was doing right now, looking for evidence of whoever had trespassed on her property and abandoned a little baby.

They were examining the shrub that had gotten everyone so worried about Angel earlier. In a police force as small as the one in Jasper, with fewer than a dozen officers, they all wore many hats. And today, apparently it was Cal's and Jason's turns to be evidence technicians. Or, more likely, it was Jason's turn, but Cal came along because he was better than anyone else at training new hires. And he enjoyed it. He'd likely volunteered to come out to DCA when dispatch sent Jason as Macon's backup.

"Cal," she called out. "The house key is on one of the wall hooks just past the front door. I'm sure Jason remembers which one to use. But I doubt you'll need it. DCA's manager, Barbara Macy, should be here soon. She'll take care of the place. Will you update her please, let her know why I'm not here?"

"No worries. Gotcha covered," he called back, not turning around. He was too intent on keeping an eye on Jason as the much younger officer used his gloved hand to carefully slide the piece of torn blanket into a paper evidence bag.

A shiver shot through her as she pictured someone hiding in those bushes, waiting. How long had they been there, watching her house?

"Emma?" Macon asked. "Are you okay?"

She forced the disconcerting image away and hurried to the passenger side of Macon's SUV, where he stood waiting with the door open. "I'm good." She motioned to Bogie in the back seat. "What about him? I don't think they'll want him inside the hospital."

"We'll drop him off at my place. It's on the way. Won't take but a minute."

"Your place?"

"A rental just outside of town, about a mile from the hospital."

"Then you really have left Boise? You're here to stay, not temporarily on loan to the department, like a task force?"

He studied her a moment. Something dark flickered in his light brown eyes, something she couldn't quite read. Was it sadness? Or something else?

"I'm not sure for how long," he said. "But yes, for now, I'm staying."

For now. She wondered why he'd come back if he didn't know his long-term plans. Did it have to do with that look she'd seen?

She climbed up into the passenger seat and he closed her door. As he rounded the hood, he stopped to answer a question Cal asked him. She took advantage of the opportunity to admire his muscular build, those sexy biceps and long legs that she remembered so well. His six-foot-three height had even made her, at five foot seven, feel petite and extra feminine. His brown hair was the same as she remembered too, kept stylishly sideswept on the top with a fade on the side. But it was his gorgeous smile she'd always appreciated the most, framed by the light barely-there beard he sported.

That smile had been displayed quite a lot as they'd bantered back and forth for the weeks when he was here for training, both him and his K-9 partner, Bogie. She'd felt safe flirting with Macon, knowing that he'd return to Boise once the training was over and she wouldn't see him again. And now here he was, here for good. Or for however long he decided to stay. That could have been a problem if he'd walked in expecting to capitalize on all that flirting, to try to build a deeper relationship when she didn't know if she'd ever be ready for something like that, with anyone. But she didn't think she needed to worry. Nothing about him gave her the impression he even remembered that they'd ever flirted.

This Macon was different.

He seemed far more serious and quiet than he'd been over two years ago. Of course, a lot could take place in two years. Had something bad happened with his job? Was that what had put that indecipherable dark look in his gaze? Or was it his personal life that had changed him? Family troubles? Girlfriend troubles?

That last thought had her sobering. Did he have a girlfriend now? And why did that possibility bother her when she wasn't interested in that kind of relationship? She wasn't good at relationships. Someone always got hurt, and that someone was usually her.

The driver's-side door opened and he hopped

inside. "Seat belt," he reminded her, as he put his own on and then started the engine.

As soon as her belt was clicked into place, he sped down the driveway.

When he pulled off the road a few minutes later, he parked in front of a faded white cottage that looked even smaller than her ranch house. She'd probably passed it a hundred times and never even knew it was here, hidden around a slight curve in the road, with thick trees sheltering it from view.

She was relieved that he didn't ask her to come inside, even though she was curious to see it. But she was more anxious to get to the hospital. Even though Angel wasn't hers, or her responsibility at this point, she had to see for herself that the baby girl was okay. Maybe it was because of what she and her siblings had gone through when they were little. She couldn't stand the idea of not knowing for sure that Angel was going to be taken care of, that she wouldn't be dumped again on someone's porch without any concern for the weather or coyotes or other critters that could have hurt her when she was outside all alone.

True to his word, it only took Macon a few minutes to secure Bogie and get back in the SUV. He was on the phone when he got inside, barely glancing at her before pulling onto the road and speeding toward Memorial Hospital.

When they parked in a space near the emergency room, he ended the call and gave her his full attention. "That was DCF, the Department of Child and

Family Services. They don't have any foster families available here in Jasper. And none of their caseworkers in Payette or Grangeville are available right now, so they're going to send one from the Boise office."

"Boise? That's three hours south of us."

"Might take even longer than that. They're scrambling to find a caseworker to come all the way to Jasper, not to mention line up a foster family who can fit one more child into an already full home. Seems like far more kids need help than there are homes and qualified people willing to take them in."

A twinge of guilt shot through her. But she ruthlessly shoved it away. She'd already done her fair share, fostered plenty of kids over the years. And while it had been incredibly rewarding, the emotional toll was overwhelming. Every time one of her foster kids was adopted or reunited with their birth family, a piece of her heart went with them. She didn't want to go through that again. That part of her life was over.

"Angel's a helpless little baby," she argued. "She can't be *fit in* with a family who already has all the kids they can handle. She needs someone who can devote time to her, give her the security and attention a baby needs."

He arched a brow. "Are you volunteering?"

She blinked. "What? No. No, no, no. I don't foster."

"But you have, in the past. Didn't you tell me you'd fostered nearly a dozen kids over the years? I know you fostered Jason Wright. Now he's a rookie police officer. You obviously did right by him. Are you still licensed with Family Services?"

She shook her head. "No. I mean, yes, I've kept my license current but I haven't fostered in years. The only reason my license is active is for emergency situations, if a child is in desperate need and there's no one to take them in—for a very limited time."

"This seems like an emergency to me."

"I meant emergencies for *older* kids, teens. I've never taken in a baby. I wouldn't. I couldn't. I'm not qualified."

"You seemed plenty qualified when you were taking care of Angel at your house."

"That's…that's different. It was…temporary. Like…taking care of a wounded animal. The basics. Food, warmth, reassurance. I wouldn't know what to do going forward. And why are we even discussing this? I don't have a crib or any of the baby things she'd need." She opened the passenger door. "Shouldn't we hurry? The doctor might be waiting to talk to us. And I don't want Angel left alone while waiting for Child Services to get here."

Cutting off any chance of him trying to convince her to foster Angel, she hopped out of the SUV and took off toward the emergency room.

Chapter Four

He'd spooked her. Macon stretched his legs out in front of him and shifted in the too-narrow, barely padded wooden chair as he studied Emma across from him in the ER waiting room.

Other than giving him her official statement about what had happened, she'd hardly looked at him since. It had taken quite a bit of prodding for her to even admit there were some people she didn't know well who'd been working at DCA recently. William Shrader, Hugh Engel, and Kyle Novell were exactly the kind of troubled teens Macon wanted to check out in relation to Angel being dumped on Emma's doorstep. But she hadn't been pleased when he'd said he'd have to interview them to see if they had alibis. That was nearly two hours ago. Now he and Emma were stuck waiting for the young woman at the information desk to let them know when the doctor finished examining the baby. Apparently, the ER was short-staffed today. Macon didn't even know whether the doctor had seen Angel yet.

He glanced at Emma. As anxious as he was for the update about the baby, he was just as anxious to know whether Emma was uncomfortable around him because his showing up was so unexpected, or if she was worried he was going to try to talk her into fostering Angel again.

Uncomfortable was never something they'd been with each other in the past. The smiles, the laughter, had come easily between them. He hadn't missed the fact that she didn't laugh or smile as easily around anyone else. It had given him hope that maybe she'd been as attracted to him as he was to her. But then the training sessions were over. He and Bogie were both deemed ready to return to his K-9 task force in Boise.

Short of quitting his job, there really wasn't any reason to push for something more between them at that point, regardless of how much he'd wanted it. A long-distance relationship hadn't made sense considering there was a zero percent chance that she'd ever sell her ranch or he'd quit his job and move.

He sighed heavily and leaned back. So much for that zero percent chance. Here he was, living in Jasper. But after what had happened in Boise, he could no longer stay there. He'd had to leave, for his own sanity. And coming here had seemed the logical choice. He liked this sleepy little town. Jasper was close enough to the mountains for a spectacular view. Far enough away that he didn't have to deal with the dangerous turns and steep drop-offs that could be treacherous during the winter. He much preferred town life, or at least, being a few miles outside of town. It gave him access to everything he needed. But it also gave him the privacy he craved. It was a lot easier getting through the days, and long dark nights, when he didn't have to pretend everything was okay.

His stomach chose that moment to rumble. He checked the time on his phone. This was taking forever. He needed to check in with the chief and give him an update, and find out what was going on with DCF. Maybe he'd grab a snack while he was at it.

Emma glanced at him, her blue-eyed gaze locking onto his for a moment before flitting away. Dang, she was pretty, even prettier than he remembered. As usual, she'd pulled her shoulder-length light brown hair into a ponytail to keep it out of her way. But it only served to emphasize the delicate femininity of her golden-tanned face.

Her light jacket hung open in deference to the warm waiting room. And he knew, both in his older memories and the new ones formed hours ago, that her long legs still looked great in a pair of jeans. Her narrow waist only made her curves up top all the more appealing. But it was those eyes, more than anything, that had always been her best feature. Lashes that were dark and thick without the need for makeup framed slightly tilted ice-blue eyes that mirrored the intelligence behind them, and the empathy that was as much a part of her as breathing.

Perhaps his favorite thing about those incredible eyes was that they truly were a window to her soul.

Every emotion she experienced flitted through them, like a movie playing out. Talking wasn't even necessary for him to see what she was thinking. As a cop, he was used to having people lie to him every day. It was beyond refreshing to know that he could always tell the truth about Emma just by looking in those expressive, gorgeous eyes.

She glanced at him again, then frowned. "Why are you smiling?"

"I'm not supposed to smile?"

"I didn't say that."

He chuckled and stood. "I'm going to grab us something from the cafeteria if it's open. Or a vending machine. Any requests? Preferences?"

She shook her head no.

"All right, be back soon."

When he returned, he divvied out the snacks and two bottles of water. She thanked him and nibbled on one of the sandwiches he'd gotten from a machine since the cafeteria had closed early, it being a Saturday. He didn't bother to tell her about the updates he'd received from his chief and Family Services. Basically, that initial inquiries had yielded no clues as to Angel's identity. And although a DCF caseworker was on his way here, no foster family had been found yet to take care of the baby.

Time seemed to drag while they waited. He checked with the volunteer at the information desk, twice, but she had no updates. The second time, when he took his seat again, he couldn't help noting how agitated Emma seemed. He leaned forward, resting his forearms on his knees. "She's going to be okay. Try not to worry."

"Who said I was worried?"

Your eyes said it. But instead of telling her that, he simply shrugged.

She didn't deny that she was concerned. Which was another thing he liked about her. Honesty. What she didn't want you to know, she wouldn't talk about. But she wouldn't lie about it. Some might call that lying by omission. He figured she was entitled to her privacy. It almost made him feel guilty that he could read her emotions so easily, even when she was trying to hide them.

"You're doing it again," she accused.

"What?"

"Smiling. Not that there's anything wrong with that. I just…"

"You just?"

"Well…you used to smile all the time. But you smiling now, it's one of the few times since I've seen you again that I've noticed you smile. I guess I was just wondering why you stopped smiling so much."

Her words evoked the images he was trying so hard to keep locked away.

Her hand was suddenly on his as she leaned across the space between their chairs. "I'm sorry. Whatever it is, it's none of my business. I shouldn't have pried."

Unable to resist the impulse, he turned his hand beneath hers, lacing their fingers together. When she didn't pull away, something like relief swept through him. He'd missed her, their closeness, their easy friendship teetering on something deeper, richer. And, until now, he hadn't realized just how much he'd missed something as simple as holding someone's hand, of holding *Emma's* hand.

"It's okay," he told her. "It's not a secret, really. It was in the news all over Boise."

She blinked. "In the news?"

He nodded. "The K-9 task force Bogie and I were on, we ran into some trouble at the culmination of an investigation. We had over twenty officers and K-9s at a warehouse to swoop in and arrest the ring of criminals we were after. Everything was planned down to the minute. But…some things you can't plan for. Like a hidden room that our confidential informants didn't know about, that wasn't in the building's blueprints."

"Oh no."

"Oh no is right. Everyone had been arrested and was being taken outside when Bogie and Nemo, my human partner's dog, alerted to a sound behind us."

"Wait. Your human partner? Are you talking about Ken Bianca, the guy I met a few years ago when he came to DCA to check on your training?"

He nodded. "Nemo was Ken's K-9. They were both with me that day. Bullets were flying before we could even turn around. Three more thugs had been hiding in the room and thought the building had been emptied out. When they slid the door open and saw us, they panicked, started shooting. It was a disaster."

Her eyes widened and her gaze slid down his body as if searching for injuries. "Did you get hit?"

"Almost. If the bullet had gone to the left just a few more inches, it would have been me who died that day."

She blinked again. "Oh no. Ken?"

He nodded again, his throat tight.

She squeezed his hand tighter in hers. "Macon, I'm so sorry. Ken seemed like such a nice guy."

"He was."

"That's such an awful tragedy. I really am sorry. But I'm glad you're okay."

He gently tugged his hand free and sat back, feeling awkward being comforted when he felt guilty for even being alive. "Hard to believe it's already been six months."

"Was Ken married? Did he have kids?"

"Divorced. No kids. I guess in a way that's a blessing, that a wife and kids weren't left behind. But he had a huge family, five siblings, tons of aunts, uncles, cousins. His parents are still around, too. They were devastated, of course. They never expected to bury one of their children."

He forced a smile, pushing hard at the darkness that wanted to settle over him. "Boise's a big city, but I lived on the same street as Ken's parents and two of his sisters. We ran into each other all the time. They were gracious, always nice, never blamed me for what happened. But I could see the truth in their eyes, that they wished it had been the other way around, that Ken had lived." He cleared his throat. "It was too hard, on all of us."

"That's why you left. Survivor's guilt."

"That's one way to put it, I guess. But there was another reason, too."

"Oh? What's that?"

You. That thought surprised him, but as soon as it occurred to him, he knew it was true. Part of the reason he'd returned to Jasper was the hope of seeing Emma again. Not to try to rekindle their fledgling relationship. He was too much of a wreck for that. But seeing a friendly face, someone who didn't look at him and wish he could trade places with their dead relative, was something he'd craved.

"Bogie," he finally answered. "I think he's got some PTSD or something, over the shooting. Sometimes he can be skittish. He's lost confidence, startles easily. Before all of this happened today, I was planning on dropping in sometime soon to let you know I was back in town. And I was going to ask if you'd be interested in working with Bogie again to help him out. Chief Walters already agreed, said the K-9 training fund at the station would pick up the tab for at least some training, when I have time to bring him by of course and in between callouts, or maybe training in the evenings if that's an option. Thankfully the chief didn't listen to Captain Arthur Rutledge, his second-in-command. As usual he was against everything to do with DCA and recommended against paying for any training."

She shook her head. "I've only met him a few times but I've heard how anti-K-9 program he is. I can't understand why he's so against it."

"Maybe he got bitten by a dog when he was a kid and can't get beyond it."

She laughed. "Maybe so."

"Anyway, I'm hoping we can work the training in as I get time. That is, if *you* have time."

"I'm pretty busy these days, with a full kennel right now."

Disappointment shot through him. "No problem. It's not an emergency or anything. The chief isn't relying on Bogie. He's letting him come up to speed gradually. I just thought—"

"You thought right. That I'd want to help him. And I do. Like I said, my schedule is really full. But I'll make adjustments, move things around. You said it's been six months since the shooting?"

He nodded.

"Then we need to get Bogie training again right away. That's a long time for him to be anxious and out of sorts. We need to rebuild his confidence as soon as possible." She cocked her head, studying him. "And yours."

"Um, mine?"

"Whether you want to admit it or not, you're probably suffering from some PTSD yourself or you wouldn't have left Boise and everything you'd worked for there. I remember that being your dream job. You need some retraining too, time to refocus and build your confidence along with your K-9 partner."

He crossed his arms. "I'm fine."

She gave him a doubtful look. "I'm not a head doctor. I won't press the issue. But I do hope that if you haven't seen anyone for what you went through, that you do soon. The problems you see manifesting in Bogie's behavior can manifest in your own life as well, whether you realize it or not."

"Obviously Chief Walters doesn't agree with you. He hired me without stipulations or reservations."

"As far as you know."

He stiffened.

"You said he's letting Bogie come up to speed slowly. You sure you're not included in that assessment?"

Before he could respond, she held up her hands in a placating gesture. "That was out of line. I'm sorry. Not trying to start an argument. I just want to make sure you and Bogie are both okay. Fair enough?"

He blew out a long breath and forced himself to relax. "Fair enough."

"Good. Then I'll expect you and Bogie both to come in for retraining, starting next week if that's okay with the chief."

"Next week as in this Monday? Two days from now?"

She nodded. "That gives me the weekend to rearrange my schedule, call in some favors from some other K-9 training facilities to help take on some of the load I have."

"I don't want to interfere with your previous obligations. Or cause you to lose income by switching things around."

"I appreciate that, but you don't need to worry. Things are good at DCA. And between the money my mom got when dad was killed on duty, and the investments she left me, I'm set. I'm not exactly buying Gucci purses or a Maserati. But I have everything I need. Besides, if you don't agree to show up sometime Monday for training, you'll hurt my feelings. You wouldn't want to do that, would you?"

He couldn't help but smile at her teasing. "No, I wouldn't want to hurt your feelings. That's for sure."

She slapped her hands on the tops of her thighs. "Good. It's settled. We'll—"

"Officer Ridley? Ms. Daniels?" The volunteer from the information desk in the waiting room approached them. "You're here for Baby Jane Doe, correct?"

"Angel," Emma corrected. "Yes, we're here for her. Is she okay?"

"I don't have any information on her status, just that the doctor is ready to speak to you." She motioned toward one of the doors on the far side of the room. "He'll meet you in there in just a few minutes."

The fear that flared in Emma's eyes had Macon standing and holding out his hand. "Come on. Whatever happens, we'll face it together."

Relief flooded her expression as she stood. "Together." She took his hand and they headed toward the door the volunteer had indicated.

Chapter Five

"I don't understand." Emma glanced from the doctor to the nurse he'd brought with him into the little privacy room off the main waiting area. "You said Angel appears to be a healthy two-month-old baby girl, that you didn't find anything concerning. But you're admitting her overnight?"

The doctor glanced at Macon before answering. "Unless the police can figure something out around the foster situation, we don't have a choice. There's nowhere to send Baby Doe—"

"Angel," Emma insisted.

"Right. Angel. Child Services isn't here yet. We can't keep the baby in the ER waiting for them when we need the beds for others with true emergencies."

The nurse beside him smiled at Emma. "She'll be well taken care of, Ms. Daniels. She'll be in the nursery on the maternity ward."

Emma fisted her hands in her lap. "Will someone hold her? Rock her? Reassure her? Or will they only give her attention when it's time for a feeding or diaper change? No offense. But everyone seems to be short-staffed and overworked these days. And it only makes sense that if other babies have medical needs, they'll receive the bulk of the attention. But that means that Angel, who has to be feeling out of sorts having already been abandoned once, may feel abandoned again. I don't want that to happen."

She turned to Macon. "Any updates on when Child Services will arrive? And whether they've found a family to take her in?"

His apologetic expression told her the answer before he even spoke.

"It's probably still going to be a little while before a caseworker gets here. And, no, the last text I got said they haven't lined up a foster family yet."

The doctor stood to leave. "I'm sorry, Ms. Daniels. But that's the best we can do. And I need to get back to the ER."

"I know. I understand. I really do. I appreciate everything you're both doing for her," Emma said. "Can I…can we see her?"

He motioned toward the nurse. "I'll leave that to Ms. Baker." He nodded at them and stepped out.

Ms. Baker, the nurse, held the door open. "They're getting a spot ready for her upstairs in the nursery. I can bring her in here for you to say goodbye."

"Thank you. I appreciate that."

When the door closed behind the nurse, Emma said, "Stop looking at me like that, Macon."

His brows arched. "Like what?"

"Like you still think I should volunteer to foster Angel."

"Well, you would be great at it. And if you foster her, you won't have to worry about her, because you'll know she's being taken care of."

"That's just it. If I took her home, I don't know that she'll be taken care of." She clasped her hands around her waist and started pacing back and forth in the small room.

Macon sat in one of the two chairs, watching her. "Is it because of your busy schedule? You'd worry you wouldn't have enough time for her?"

She stopped in front of him, hands on her hips. "Of course I'd have time for her," she snapped. "As much as I love the dogs I'm training, people are more important. I'd make time for her."

"Then what's the issue, exactly?" He held up his hands to stop her angry retort. "I'm just playing devil's advocate, trying to understand your concerns. What has you so scared about taking care of Angel?"

She blinked, absorbing his words as she slowly sank into the other chair. "I *am* scared. You're right about that." She squeezed her eyes shut, breathing deep and even to try to calm her racing heart. The very idea of taking care of a baby, of being its foster parent, sent a cold chill through her. There were so many reasons that she'd never fostered any babies. And the very worst reason was something beyond her control—genetics.

A gentle hand lifted her chin until she was staring into Macon's light brown eyes. The kindness and empathy staring back at her almost made her lose her composure.

"Emma," he whispered, his deep voice soothing. "No pressure. Angel's going to be taken care of no matter what. But what, exactly, scares you about the thought of that person taking care of her being you?" He dropped his hand and waited, his gaze searching hers.

"Genetics," she finally blurted out. "And before you say that's crazy, I know how it sounds. But I can't help it. You know my biological parents were monsters. But the few stories I told you about them didn't begin to delve into the depth of their depravity. They were horrible, awful people. Still are, as far as I know, unless one of them has died in prison and no one told me." She shivered and rubbed her hands up and down her arms. "But the thing is, they didn't start out as monsters. I was the oldest, and I remember how it was, before my sister and brother were born. Back when my dad had a steady job, before Mom got hooked on drugs, they were nice, loving even. We had good times, good memories. But after the financial stress of two more kids, after Daddy got hurt and couldn't hold down a job anymore, and Mom turned to drugs and alcohol, they changed. Everything changed. Whatever love they'd once had died. They both became broken and took their disappointments in life out on the most innocent and vulnerable members of their family."

"Emma. You're nothing like your parents. I've seen the way you are with animals, with other people. You're empathetic and really care about them."

"My mom was loving once. How do I know I won't become like her? That the baby might cry and I get mad and—"

He took her hands in his. "Stop. It wouldn't happen. You'll never become what they became. I've seen you deal with animals who were belligerent, dangerous even. And you never raised your voice or your hand. Not once. Instead, you offered love and patience and security. And you won them over, calmed them, made them feel secure. I know you won't snap and become some awful person under extreme stress because I've *seen* you under extreme stress. You handled it far better than I ever could, than most people I know could. Genetics or not, you learned lessons from how your parents acted. You learned how it feels to be on the bad end of that, and made a point of never treating anyone, human or not, that way. You're a good person, Emma. Trust me on that."

She stared up at him, stunned at both what he'd said and the emotion behind his words. "You really believe that, don't you?"

Gently, ever so slowly, he cupped her face in his hands. "I really believe that." Then he shocked her by kissing her forehead before letting go and sitting back.

Who'd have thought a mere touch of someone's

hand on her face, and a kiss on her forehead, could send a jolt of awareness straight through her body? Wow. But that was…chemistry. There'd always been an attraction between them. It didn't mean he was right about her, about whether heredity truly mattered or not.

She shook her head, rejecting his arguments. "I appreciate your confidence, your belief in me. But I can't do it. I can't risk it. The very idea of fostering Angel is ridiculous."

He looked like he was about to argue again, but a knock sounded on the door.

"Come in," Emma called out.

The nurse pushed open the door, cradling Angel in one hand and smiling. "Here you go. I'll give you some time to say goodbye."

Before Emma could even prepare herself, the baby was thrust in her arms and the nurse left.

She stared down at the precious bundle, the dark curly hair matting the top of her head, the pink bow lips seemingly smiling in her sleep. An adhesive bandage almost bigger than her hand was taped across the back where they'd probably drawn blood. Emma gently rubbed a finger across it, hoping the little baby hadn't felt the jab of the needle.

"Macon?"

"Hmm?" He leaned across her and gently tucked the blanket around one of the baby's feet that had been poking out.

"Has anyone made any progress in finding out who she is?"

"We've barely begun the investigation at this point. But we're keeping an open mind, in spite of that note that makes it appear that her mother is the one who left her. It's also possible there was a carjacking or something like that where someone ended up with a baby and didn't know what to do and left her on your doorstep. There aren't any missing persons reports or calls about a kidnapped baby as of yet. But, again, it's early. We're reaching out to neighboring counties, seeing if they've heard anything."

"How could a baby go unaccounted for and the parents, or grandparents, or even a concerned neighbor not immediately report it to the police? It's not like she's a teenager who could have stayed after school for some kind of extra-curricular activity. Babies are always with someone. A parent would have to know she was missing. It has to be a parent who abandoned her, don't you think? If not the mother, then the father?"

He shrugged. "Seems the most likely scenario. If that's the case, something made them desperate. Otherwise, I can't see them leaving her like that. Whoever was taking care of her was doing a good job."

She looked up at him. "She is well cared for, isn't she? I mean, no bruises. She's not too thin. The doctor said she was healthy."

He nodded. "I'm guessing if it wasn't the parents who left her, then someone stole her and the parents are too scared to go to the police—like if they're undocumented and are afraid they might be deported. Or..."

"Or?"

"Or, maybe they're down on their luck, unable to take care of Angel the way they want to and know you, or have heard about you. Maybe they left her on your porch hoping you'd take care of her, because they trust you."

She stared at him, shocked. "They trust me? So they left her there? Where a coyote could have come up on the porch and hurt her?"

"Maybe they were waiting for you to get her, and they were crouched in those bushes watching over her, ready to step in if a wild animal came along. The blood on the leaves tells us someone was there."

"I'm guessing it will take a while to trace the blood?"

"I wouldn't pin my hopes on anything useful any time soon. Getting a DNA profile can take weeks or longer, depending on the state lab's backlog."

"Weeks? Or longer?"

"Most likely, yes. And even with a profile, unless the contributor of that blood sample has committed a felony in the past and their DNA is in the databases, it won't do us any good. We're looking into those three teens you mentioned who work part-time at DCA so we can determine whether they're involved in some way. If any of them seem promising, I'll push the chief to try to get them to submit DNA samples to match against. It's expensive, though, and without probable cause we won't be able to force them to submit to the test. But we'll explore that angle and see where it leads."

She nodded. "They were the first ones I thought of when I found Angel. But it doesn't really make sense. They're so young. And I haven't heard about any of them even having a girlfriend. I sincerely doubt the baby is one of theirs."

"You know them well enough to know about potential girlfriends?"

"Well, no. Not really. I barely know them if I'm being completely honest here."

"How often do they come to DCA?"

"Two to three afternoons a week. They're all three seniors and only need a few classes to graduate high school. So they have early release. Kyle and Hugh usually show up in the early afternoon on Thursdays and Fridays. William is more sporadic because of extracurricular activities at school."

"I'll look into each of their backgrounds, see what I can find. In the meantime, someone needs to step up to take care of Angel."

She shook her head. "Even if you're right that someone trusts me and that's why they left her on my doorstep, it doesn't matter. What do I know about taking care of a baby? Nothing. I've never fostered anyone but teens. And it's not like I've got siblings and nieces and nephews to practice on. Rick and

Susan showed me love, gave me role models for how to care for older kids, for other people. But babies?" She shook her head. "Never. Before this morning, I'd never even changed a diaper."

"I have."

She jerked her head up. "You've changed a diaper?"

He nodded. "I come from a large family, plenty of nieces and nephews. And I'm the oldest. I babysat my younger siblings hundreds of times. I could give you some pointers to try to avoid some messy leaks."

"No." She shook her head. "No, I told you. I'm not qualified. There has to be someone else better at this, someone who can take care of her."

He placed a hand on her arm. "It's okay, Emma. You don't have to explain, or feel guilty about not taking her in. DCF will see that she's taken care of. She'll be okay."

A tear traced down her cheek. She wiped it away and stared down at the delicate face so content and happy-looking in sleep.

Another knock sounded on the door. The nurse must have come back to take Angel upstairs.

"Are you ready?" Macon asked, hand on the doorknob, prepared to open it.

She stiffened her back, gave him a crisp nod. "Ready."

He opened the door. But instead of the nurse, there was a man standing there. He was slightly balding and about a foot shorter than Macon, with a rumpled dress shirt tucked into a pair of faded jeans. The badge hanging on a lanyard around his neck probably showed his name, but it was too small for Emma to read. The three large letters stamped across the front, however, weren't. They read DCF.

She swallowed, automatically clutching Angel tighter as the man shook hands with Macon and they discussed the baby's situation.

A moment later, the nurse appeared behind them with another nurse who was wearing yellow scrubs with little ducks and bunnies all over them. And she was holding an infant carrier. They were here to take Angel upstairs to the maternity ward.

Where she'd be placed in a bassinet and left alone while the nurses tended to the other babies who needed medical attention.

The little room went silent. Emma realized they were all watching her.

"Ma'am," the nurse in yellow scrubs said. "I'm ready to take her." She held her hands out, smiling reassuringly.

Emma kissed Angel's cheek, then held her out toward the nurse, all the while trying to ignore the hot tears coursing down her face.

But just as the nurse started to take her, Emma snatched her back. "I've changed my mind. I'm keeping her." She grabbed her purse and took off down the hallway.

Chapter Six

"I'm keeping her?" Macon grinned at Emma in his SUV's rearview mirror as she rode beside the infant carrier holding Angel.

Her face turned a delightful shade of pink. "I just meant that I'd foster her, of course. Until they can find her rightful parents. Or another foster family to take her in."

"Lucky for you, Mr. Burns didn't call the police to swear out a complaint on behalf of DCF that you'd kidnapped her when you took off."

She rolled her eyes. "The police, *you*, were already there. And I didn't kidnap her. I just took her to the car to wait while you handled the paperwork."

He laughed but let it drop. It had taken considerably more than *paperwork* for him to calm everyone down when Emma ran off with Angel. The DCF caseworker had been livid and wanted her arrested, particularly since he'd driven four hours from his home to officially take custody of the baby and sign her in to the hospital until the desired foster family could be found. After Macon had told him Emma was a registered foster parent, and he'd explained Emma's background, just enough to gain some empathy from the caseworker, his anger had cooled. And then once Macon pointed out that DCF wouldn't have to pay for an overnight hospital stay, and that the caseworker no longer had to find an emergency foster placement, he'd ended up smiling and in a good mood. He'd signed on the dotted line so fast he'd almost forgotten to get Emma's signature. He'd transferred the infant car seat he'd brought to Macon's SUV, had Emma sign some forms, then took off, eager to head home.

"This is crazy," Emma said from the back seat. "I don't even have a crib. No diapers, no formula, well, except for what was left on my porch in that pink bag. What was I thinking?"

"You were thinking that you were the best option for little Angel right now. And I agree with you. As to the rest, that's being taken care of. There's a foster closet here in town."

"A foster what?"

"Closet. It's fairly new, no doubt created after you last fostered. It's a charity that works with DCF to help foster families get the supplies they need. The foster families exchange gently used clothing through the closet to other foster families. Donations of food and supplies, even furniture—like cribs and beds— are made by churches and others wanting to help. The caseworker, Mr. Burns, already put the call out.

Someone from the foster closet is gathering up things for little Angel right now. They'll bring everything by later today."

"That's amazing. I always wondered how other foster parents were able to afford the clothes, games, food, everything you need when fostering. It's a struggle, even when you're doing okay financially like me. Goodness knows what DCF pays doesn't come close to covering expenses."

"Which makes it even more amazing that people like you agree to help."

"Stop. You're making me out to be a saint or something. Trust me. I'm far from it. If anything, I'm being selfish."

"Selfish? How?" He passed a slow-moving car and moved back into his lane.

"I'm in it for the rewards, like Angel's smiles when she looks up at me. I can't explain it. It just…it just feels so good to hold her, to see her happy."

"She's really too young to actually smile. It's probably gas."

She rolled her eyes again. "That's ridiculous. Of course she smiles. Besides, who made you the baby expert?"

"Younger siblings, and nieces and nephews, remember? If you ever need a break from watching her, I could help. As long as I'm not working a shift at the station, of course."

"Are you serious? You'd babysit her?"

"You don't have to act so surprised. I like kids,

babies. Besides, you'll need me to show you how to change a diaper. I guess it's my turn to train you."

She laughed. "I guess it is. But Piper and Barb will help too. I texted them when you were talking to Mr. Burns. They both said they'd come over sometime this weekend to see her. Hey, wait, didn't we just pass your house?"

"I'm taking you straight to the ranch. No need to stop."

"What about Bogie? Won't he need to go out? We were at the hospital for several hours."

"There's a dog door. The back yard's fenced. He'll be okay, probably will sleep most of the time anyway."

A few minutes later, they turned into her long driveway. He glanced in the mirror at her and noticed her smiling at the metal cutout of a German shepherd on top of the arch over the entrance. He remembered her telling him once that it was supposed to be Duke, the K-9 cop partner of her father who'd been killed the same night as him. He'd expected that the daily reminder of her father would make her sad. But she'd explained to him it did just the opposite. It reminded her how blessed she'd been to be taken in by Rick and Susan Daniels.

A flash of orange off to his left disappeared so quickly into the trees that he half wondered whether he'd imagined it. But it was likely to be old Gus, the half-feral orange-and-white tabby who reigned supreme over the Daniels Canine Academy. Emma and a few others could occasionally pet him, but never pick him up. The closest Macon had ever gotten to Gus was a fly-by brush-up against his legs as the cat took off in search of his next meal. Not that he ever went hungry. Emma always made sure to keep fresh food and water in the outbuildings for him. But Gus reveled in the hunt. He preferred the kind of meals that squeaked and ran.

Now that he had time to really take things in, without being on the alert for a bad guy, Macon drank in the pristine, well-kept ranch as he drove up the long driveway. There were two familiar-looking cars parked to the left of the kennels by Emma's old pickup. Her friends had obviously made good already on their promise to come over this weekend and were likely waiting inside the house.

Piper Lambert's car was on the far left. Piper had been Emma's friend since college and had started helping her train dogs about four years ago. The other car belonged to Barbara Macy. Barb helped with paperwork, managing the business, and some light cleaning. He remembered she'd also been in charge of managing any volunteers who came out to DCA to socialize new pups or clean the kennels.

DCA was a fixture and well-liked by the little town of Jasper, Idaho. Especially since Emma ensured the small police force had the best-trained K-9s around—K-9s they couldn't even afford if it weren't for her generosity and her network of animal lovers around the state who donated to the cause.

Nothing much seemed to have changed, except

himself. He definitely wasn't the man he used to be. When staying in Boise had become too painful, impossible to endure, he'd been desperate to escape. When he'd tried to figure out where to go, a place that was warm, welcoming, friendly but not intrusive, a name kept whispering through his mind—Jasper. And right on its heels was another name.

Emma.

He had no misconceptions that he was about to kindle anything romantic between them. He was too broken for that. But his battered soul craved a glimpse of her warm smile, and the easy friendship they'd once shared, if only for a little while. He'd been gifted with a few of those smiles at the hospital. But with a baby in the mix now, he imagined that would be it for a very long time. Emma was about to have her hands full. There'd be little time for a damaged cop who might or might not have the potential for something more in her life.

He pulled to a stop in the circular drive in front of her house, noting the absence of other police vehicles. Cal and Jason must have collected all the evidence they could find and left.

Emma was forced to wait for him to open the back door since it couldn't be opened from the inside. She smiled her thanks as he lifted out the infant in her carrier and brought everything up the stairs.

The door burst open and suddenly Emma and the baby were surrounded by Piper and Barb excitedly chattering and oohing and aahing over the baby.

Everyone was pretty much ignoring Macon, so he leaned against one of the posts that held up the roof over the porch and crossed his arms, waiting. As he watched Emma, he was sucker-punched all over again. *This* Emma, the one who was so happy and carefree, enamored with a newborn, had his heart thumping in his chest. Every cell in his body was tingling and buzzing, as if he was coming out of a deep freeze and sparking back to life.

At thirty-one, Emma could still pass for a college kid. If people in town didn't know her so well, they'd be asking to see her ID before selling her any alcohol. When his former partner from Boise had briefly met Emma when he'd traveled to DCA to check on Macon's training progress, he'd teased Macon that he'd finally found someone tall enough that she'd fit under his shoulder if they stood beside each other. Not that Emma was all that tall, but she was taller than average and Macon was a good six foot three. Ken had been right. She matched him perfectly, in a lot of ways.

Like him, she took care of herself, but not by working out in a gym. She had a lithe, toned body from her hard work on the ranch. And sun-kissed light brown hair that bounced behind her in a ponytail most days. Plus blue eyes that rivaled the blue of the skies over the Salmon River Mountains visible in the distance. But even more than her physical presence, it was her intelligence that drew him in. It was her quick wit, tenacity and soft heart that had him thinking about her long after he'd gone home to Boise, three hours south of Jasper.

He'd missed her even more than he'd realized.

Piper pulled the front door open for Barbara, who was now holding Angel. The three women rushed inside, their faces alight with excitement.

Macon grinned. Apparently Emma had forgotten he was here. The others were too smitten with the baby to notice or care. If that wasn't a signal for him to leave, he didn't know what was. He doubted Emma would need his help changing diapers after all, not with Piper and Barbara there to help. He'd check in with the foster closet again, make sure they were able to get everything together that Emma needed. If not, he'd head over to one of the box stores and get the rest himself after his shift was over.

He'd just started the engine when the front door burst open again. Emma came flying down the steps, her face red with embarrassment.

He rolled the window down as she reached the car.

"Macon, oh my gosh. I can't believe I was so rude and left you on the porch. I'm so sorry."

He chuckled. "Don't be. I'm glad you and your friends are enjoying Angel. You don't seem to need me right now and I have to head back anyway. I'm still on duty with a few hours left of my shift to work. I'll probably spend that writing up reports on everything that happened this morning."

She clutched the windowsill of his door, her eyes searching his. "You're wrong, you know. I do need you. I needed you so much today. And I appreciate everything you did. Maybe you can type up those reports some other time and come on inside? Piper and Barbara feel bad for ignoring you, too. Let us make it up to you. I'll cook dinner."

"That's a tempting offer. Rain check? Those reports really can't wait. The team will need the information for the investigation. And after that, I should head home. Bogie's going to eat my couch if I don't feed him soon."

She smiled. "Well, why didn't you say the life of your couch was at stake? Go. I wouldn't want to be responsible for its demise." She cocked her head in that way that was always so endearing. "You *are* coming back Monday, right? You and Bogie?"

"We'll be here, either before my shift or after, depending on the workload at the station. What time do you prefer?"

"The morning, if you can swing it. Ten o'clockish for our first lesson. Eight thirty if you want breakfast."

He grinned. "I'll move mountains to get here at eight thirty." He sobered. "Emma, I live just a few miles away. If you see or hear anything, anything at all that gives you cause for concern, don't hesitate to call me. Day or night. Doesn't matter what time. Okay?"

She nodded. "If it was just me, I wouldn't even think of bothering you like that. But with Angel as my responsibility, I wouldn't want to risk *not* calling if something happens."

"It's not a bother. Call me. I mean it. Day or night. Besides, I still need to give you my best diaper-changing tips at some point."

She laughed. "Okay. But it would help if I had your number."

"I guess it would." He pulled his phone out of his pocket. "I'll call your number since I got it from the report you gave me."

Her phone rang and she saved the incoming number. "Got it. Thanks. Oh, and Macon?"

"Yeah?"

"I really am sorry about your partner, Ken. But I'm glad you're here, that you came back to Jasper." With that, she turned and hurried up the steps and into the house, her sexy ponytail waving at him like a red flag at a bull.

Macon grinned, but then the bush where they'd found the blood sample caught his attention. It was too thick, too large and far too close to the foundation of the porch. Someone could be hiding there right now and he doubted that he'd see them. He'd have to talk to Emma about trimming back the bushes the next time he saw her.

He scanned the house, the outbuildings. But even though he didn't see any signs that someone was skulking around, he couldn't shake the feeling of unease as he drove down the driveway.

Chapter Seven

Macon pulled into the circular drive promptly at eight thirty on Monday morning. Emma was sitting in one of the rocking chairs on the front porch, smiling down at him. Angel wasn't with her. She was probably inside, being cuddled by Piper or Barbara since both of their cars were parked off to the left by the kennels.

Man, she sure looked good.

Clearing his tight throat, he stepped out of the car and glanced across the SUV's roof toward her as he opened the rear door.

Bogie leaped out, a blur of black fur and rabbit-worthy ears as the shepherd bounded around the vehicle toward the porch.

"Bogie, halt," he ordered, stopping the shepherd in his tracks near the bottom step. The dog stared adoringly up at Emma, but true to his training, other than his wagging tail, he didn't move.

Macon stopped beside him, resting a boot on the bottom step as he rubbed the top of Bogie's head. "Good morning, Emma."

She looked a bit overwhelmed, but also happy to see him. Or maybe it was his dog she was happy to see.

"Macon." Her smile widened. "And Bogart. One of my most favorite pupils ever."

"And here I thought I was your favorite," Macon teased. "How'd the weekend go? Are you worn out from midnight feedings yet?"

"Oh goodness, Angel isn't *that* little. The doctor estimated she was two months old, give or take. She sleeps through the night like the angel that she is. But I haven't been taking care of her all by myself. Piper and Barbara have been unbelievable, showing me the basics, how to change diapers without them leaking everywhere, giving me tons of useful tips. Barbara's daughter, Samantha, is grown and in college but she remembers plenty about taking care of babies. And even though Piper doesn't have any kids yet, she's babysat enough for friends and relatives that she seems like an expert to me. They were both here off and on this past weekend helping me. Barbara's inside with her right now. I'm building my confidence. Might even be able to go solo in a few days. Well, except for when I'm working. Barbara is going to use my guest room as her office for a while instead of using the office in the kennel building. That way she can alternate between management duties and watching over Angel when Piper and I are with the dogs. I think it's going to work out really well."

"Sounds like it. Were you able to lighten your training load like you hoped?"

"Barbara took care of that too already. Normally, she and Piper don't work here on weekends but she dove right in, contacting other K-9 training facilities. She off-loaded a third of our dogs to them and the clients were very understanding." She motioned toward his uniform. "I forgot to ask you how long you've been a Jasper policeman."

"I'm an old-timer. Been here a whole week."

She blinked. "A week. Wait, no way. Even transferring in from Boise, you'd still have to go through the academy here, wouldn't you? And you're a lieutenant, too, if I'm understanding the insignia on your uniform correctly. I would have thought you'd have to work your way up, prove you know the Jasper PD way of doing things before you made that rank."

He smiled. "Your foster dad taught you well about how police departments work."

She gave a little laugh. "He tried. But it was Chief Walters, *Officer* Walters back then, who taught me way more than I ever wanted to know about the police. Doing my community service at the police station kept me out of juvie, so I've got nothing to complain about."

He grinned. "I still can't imagine you as a juvenile delinquent."

"Yes, well. I didn't cope well after Dad's death and rebelled. I hung out with the local bad boy, Billy, and did some pretty awful things. I was as horrible as teenagers get. And so very lucky to have someone like the chief to straighten me out and remind me who

I was, the adopted daughter of an amazing woman and her police officer husband who didn't deserve to have his memory tarnished with a daughter who was a budding criminal." She waved her hand again. "Sorry. Tripping down memory lane."

"I don't mind. And you're right about how police departments work. Normally someone transferring in would have to go through the usual training and start lower in the ranks than I did. But Chief Walters made an exception because of my previous experience working with Jasper officers as part of the task force. It also didn't hurt that I had outstanding recommendations from my boss, and Walters had a soft spot for Bogie."

She laughed. "I can see Bogie tilting things in your favor, especially since the chief is such a huge supporter of having K-9s for every Jasper officer who wants one. I'm glad you didn't have to start from the bottom. And speaking of Bogie, poor little guy is dying to say hello. Release the hounds, Macon."

"You asked for it." He gave Bogie a command in German. The shepherd instantly bounded up the steps and skidded to a tail-wagging halt in front of Emma, excited to see her but too well-trained to jump on her like another dog might have done.

She knelt down and hugged him around the neck, ruffling his fur as he wiggled like a little puppy in her grasp.

"Have one of your own yet?" he asked as he climbed the steps and stopped a few feet away.

She gave Bogie one last pat and stood. "No reason to. My kennels are full of fur babies to love on. And as it is, I barely have enough time to give my horse rescues the attention they deserve. And Gus too, when he deems that I'm allowed to see him."

He chuckled. "I thought I saw a flash of that old orange cat heading into the trees when I was here Saturday. Wasn't sure if he was still around."

"Oh he's a fixture at DCA. And the way everyone caters to his every whim, trying to get him to let them pet him, he glories in the attention."

"You're still the only one who can get near him?"

"Pretty much." She cocked her head. "And you too, if I remember right."

"Yeah, well. He's rubbed against my legs before but that's as close as he'd let me get."

"Closer than most. Even Piper can't pet him and she's a wonder with all the other animals, feeding them, helping me with training. She and Barbara are my right and left hands around here." She crossed her arms, pulling her light jacket closed against the cool breeze that was much warmer than over the weekend. It would be in the midseventies by later in the afternoon. "Got any news about the investigation? I mean, if you had a chance to get an update on it before coming out here with Bogie."

"Since I'm the lead detective on this case, I definitely am in the loop on what everyone's doing."

"Lead detective? Really?"

He grinned. "It's not as impressive as it might

sound. Jasper's so small we're basically *all* detectives, or evidence technicians as needed. Well, except the brand-new rookies like Jason. He's still in training. Otherwise, if we're the first to respond to a call from dispatch, it's our case. I've got some of the other officers digging into this one and keeping me posted. We've been meeting every morning to share status and brainstorm. I'll head over there to meet with them after we're done here." He leaned back against one of the thick wood posts on the porch. "As to what we've found out so far, not much. But not for lack of trying. The chief's all in on this one, approving shifts around the clock to figure out the baby's legal name, who her parents are. He's got a soft spot for kids. And you."

"The feeling's mutual. He's like a father to me." Her mouth turned down. "I don't count my bio dad anymore. Rick Daniels was my true father. Chief Walters is my bonus dad."

"Bonus dad. I like that. You could do much worse. He's a great guy. He did a lot of the searching himself into missing persons reports. Heck, even anti-DCA Captain Rutledge did some digging to help us out."

"I guess he's human after all, in spite of the rumors," she teased.

He smiled. "I combed through the database of the National Center for Missing and Exploited Children yesterday, trying to find a match. Nothing came close. Still no local missing persons reports. There's nothing logged in the entire state of Idaho for a baby girl her age with dark hair and dark eyes."

"Did you notice the birthmark on her upper right arm? It's an oval about the size of a quarter with ragged edges. That might help."

He nodded. "It was in the doctor's report from the ER. We included that in the flyers."

"Flyers?"

"Around town, and the neighboring counties. Next time you're in Jasper you'll see them. They're in store front windows, on lamp poles, restaurants. If she's from around here, someone's going to see her face and call it in. It's just a matter of time."

"I hope so."

"Your sad face doesn't match those words."

Her eyes widened. "Oh. Well, I mean I really do hope someone recognizes her because she needs to be with her family."

"I sense a but."

She idly patted Bogie's head; he was practically glued to her thighs, his muzzle tilted up to watch her. "Speaking from personal experience, just because someone's family, doesn't mean they're good people. If her family is who abandoned her, then I hope she doesn't go back to them."

She shook her head. "Here I am going on and on and I promised you a hot breakfast. Meanwhile it's sitting on the table getting cold. Come on. Let's eat."

He reached the door before her and held it open. She smiled her thanks and headed inside. Bogie waited for Macon's permission. Normally Macon would ask someone if it was okay for the dog to come inside. But he knew Emma would be upset if he left Bogie on the porch.

"Come on, buddy. Let's go see what's cookin'." He stepped back and the shepherd eagerly trotted inside, heading straight toward the opening to the kitchen.

Macon detoured to the sink to wash his hands, then sat at the table that dominated the little room.

Emma grimaced when the back of his chair hit the wall. "Sorry. One of these days I'm going to add on to this place, or at least expand the kitchen. It's ridiculously small."

"It's cozy. And much bigger than my rental. Besides…" He motioned toward the food she'd set out in bowls in the middle. "You won't hear me complaining when you've cooked a feast like this. If you do this every morning, I'll always make sure to stop by on my way to the office."

She laughed. "Trust me. This is a rarity, or it *was*. Dinners are easier and more my style. But since Barbara agreed to watch Angel while I'm working and had to move all her papers and supplies up here to the house, I told her one of my ways of paying her back will be to provide a hot breakfast every morning she's here. And, before you ask, she made herself a plate as the food was coming off the stove. She's eating in my guest room slash office. Totally type A, wanting to get as much work done as she can before Angel wakes up from her morning nap." She motioned toward the bowls of food. "Now go on, get yourself a plate. You'll have to nuke it in the microwave to heat it up."

"Don't have to tell me twice." He quickly piled his plate high, then took both of their plates and reheated them.

True to her word, Emma had made a mouthwatering breakfast. Scrambled eggs with cheese, fried potatoes, biscuits, gravy, and some of the best salt-cured bacon he'd ever had. Bogie seemed to agree since he got several slices in the bowl of dog food that Emma had set out just for him. Even though Macon had already fed him before leaving the house, the bacon was too much for him to resist and he happily dove into his second breakfast.

Emma laughed and smiled down at Bogie. "With that kind of appetite, I'm surprised he's not fat and lazy by now."

"He's always been food-motivated, that's for sure. Luckily he gets plenty of exercise hanging with me at work."

"Well he'll get plenty today, for sure," she said. "We'll run him through the basics again, get him used to the routine of being here. It will help build his confidence, keeping it simple. In a couple of days, we can test him on some bad-guy takedowns, see how he does."

They were both quiet for a little while as they ate. But as Macon spooned a second helping of eggs onto his plate, Emma said, "You mentioned that Bogie hesitates. To help him get past that, I need to find out what it is that's specifically giving him anxiety. As much as we love our animals and think of them as if they were little humans, it's wrong to assume that we know why they react the way they do. We have to figure out what's making him anxious, and why, before we can work to correct it. Have you noticed he balks in specific kinds of circumstances?"

He took a quick sip of coffee before answering. "Sudden, loud noises, for sure. He'll cower against me, nearly knocking me over. I have to coax and reassure him to get him to move forward. Luckily, that hasn't happened during a call here so far. But I'm only starting my second week. Everything's been smooth, quiet for the most part."

"Interesting. Have you noticed any other issues, aside from how he reacts to loud noise?"

He shrugged. "I haven't really tried to narrow it down that way. I just know that back in Boise, at least, there were a ton of times in the months following the screwup at the warehouse where he'd back up against me and refuse to move. I knew his days working there were numbered at that point. I'm not even sure he'll be able to work successfully here, but when I called Chief Walters about it, he recommended I relocate and see if you could work a miracle. So I took a chunk of my 401K to buy Bogie from Boise PD, and here I am."

She blinked. "You bought him? Jasper PD didn't buy him for you to use here?"

"The chief offered, but that kind of budget wasn't

available right away. It would have taken a while to pull the funds together. There was no guarantee what would happen to Bogie in the meantime. He wasn't fit to work in the kind of environment he'd been specifically trained for, and there really wasn't anywhere else for him there. They don't have the robust K-9 presence like we do in Jasper. They couldn't afford to let a work dog sit or gradually get back to one hundred percent. They would have sold him. I couldn't let that happen, couldn't risk him going somewhere else and me not being able to get him back."

"Police K-9s don't come cheap. That must have been a hefty hit to your investments."

He grimaced. "It hurt, no doubt about it. But Bogie was there for me more times than I can count. I wasn't going to abandon him just because it was the easier route to take."

Her eyes were suspiciously bright, as if she was holding back tears. "I sure wish there were more dog lovers like you. If there were, the pounds wouldn't be so full of neglected and abandoned animals." She rubbed the top of Bogie's head. "You're one lucky guy, sweet fella." She smiled at Macon. "As for me working a miracle with him, there aren't any miracles in what I do. Just hard work and years of experience. And if I've learned anything about K-9s, it's that you can't fix a problem if you don't know the cause. The easy explanation is that the gunshots scared him, so he's afraid of loud sounds. But working dogs like

Bogie aren't easily intimidated. I'm betting there's more to it."

She motioned toward his plate. "Take your time and eat your fill. I'm going to check on the baby, and see whether Barbara needs anything before we head outside to reacclimate Bogie to the ranch. I don't want to do too much with him the first day back. He needs to feel comfortable before we start any real training."

Macon was about to answer when the radio on his shoulder squawked. It was Jenny, the dispatcher, requesting any available units to investigate a potential break-in. When he heard the address, he glanced up at Emma. "That's a couple of miles from here."

"Go on. It's okay. Come back anytime, or we can try again tomorrow."

He shoved back from the table as he let Jenny know he'd take the call. "I'll stop by later today, for sure. Sorry about the mess. I would have helped clean up."

"I know you would." She made a shooing motion with her hands. "I understand a cop's obligations better than most. No apologies needed."

On an impulse, he leaned down and kissed her cheek. "Thanks, Emma."

For once, she was speechless, her eyes wide as she stared at him. And for once, he wasn't sure how to read her reaction. He guessed he'd figure it out later when he returned. Either she'd tell him to get lost or she'd overlook his impulsiveness. Or, if he was really lucky, she'd gladly welcome him back. He sincerely hoped it was the latter.

Chapter Eight

Emma couldn't resist one last stroke of the blood-hound's silky ears before closing the chain-link gate to his kennel. It had been a surprisingly typical Monday, long and hard getting the dogs back in the training routine after having the weekend off.

Beside her, Piper gave her a warning look. "Don't you dare try to get Red to like you more than me. I'm his favorite." She flipped her long red hair over her shoulder. "We gingers have to stick together."

Emma laughed. "No worries there. He was making puppy-dog eyes at you the whole time he drooled on me."

Piper grinned. "He's a beauty, isn't he? I think he's my favorite of the current batch of trainees. And judging by how quickly the two of you tracked and found me in the woods, I'd say he's ready to graduate."

"I was originally thinking he'd need another week. But his performance this afternoon tells me you're right. He's ready. He might be the best tracking dog we've ever worked with."

"No dog tracks better than Decoy."

Emma rolled her eyes. "You're biased since Decoy is Shane's search-and-rescue dog."

"Maybe. But I'll allow that Red has the potential to be the second-best search-and-rescue hound in this area, maybe all of Idaho."

"Says the woman who did most of his training."

Piper held her hands out in an innocent gesture. "Ain't bragging if it's true."

Emma laughed and eyed the adorable hound as he slurped from his water bowl, long ears flopping and splashing the water onto the concrete floor. "I guess it's time to notify Shane that Red's ready to join his SAR team. We'll need Red's handler here for at least a couple of hours to put them both through their final paces before Red goes home. Can you tell Barbara before you leave, get her to set it up?"

Piper moved to the sink at the end of the run to wash her hands. "I can do that now. All the training we wanted to do today is done. I've finished cleaning the kennels and feeding everyone. Nothing left to do but go home, clean the stink off and veg on the couch."

"Ha," Emma said. "I'm sure you'll be doing more than just being a couch potato with that gorgeous Shane waiting for you."

Piper sighed and dried her hands on a towel, a love-sick look on her face. "He is gorgeous, isn't he?"

"If you like the tall, buff, dark-haired type, I suppose."

"Sort of like your Lieutenant Ridley? He's taller

than Shane. And I swear his muscles have muscles. That man is *built*."

Emma arched a brow. "But he doesn't have dark hair."

They both laughed.

"See you tomorrow, boss." Piper waved and ducked out the doorway.

Emma spent a few more minutes in the kennel building, checking the gates on each dog enclosure, making sure they had clean bedding and water. But Piper was no slacker and she was doing an excellent job filling in on things Barbara normally did, in addition to Piper's regular training work. Everything was taken care of as she'd said. There was nothing else for Emma to do but check on the horses. Then she'd head inside, wash up and do what she'd been looking forward to all day—taking over babysitting duties from Barbara. She'd feed sweet little Angel her dinner and cuddle her until she fell asleep.

Gravel and dirt crunched beneath her feet as she crossed to the little barn that served as a stable and storage area. Her steps were sure and fast. She was anxious to get this last chore over with. And she couldn't lie to herself about why.

Angel.

It shocked Emma how much she enjoyed having the baby girl around, even though it had only been a few days. But she was determined not to become attached. If she did, then when they found Angel's parents, or a permanent home for her, it would break

Emma's heart. She'd already suffered too many trag-
edies in her life to risk a broken heart. Losing someone else she cared about was more pain than she was
willing to bear.

She slid open the heavy wooden barn door, then
headed inside. The late-afternoon sunlight did little
to illuminate the gloom of the interior, even with
the ventilation windows open. But with a flip of a
switch, the large overhead lights hanging down on
poles chased away the shadows.

Like her K-9 building, the barn featured a center
aisle. But where the other building had dog enclosures running down both sides, this barn was a combination of storage rooms on the right and only had
two stalls on the left. When Emma had used her in-
heritance to expand her family's property and build
DCA, she'd planned on using the barn like her father had, to store the small tractor-mower and other
equipment and tools. But when she'd found out that a
neighbor was down on their luck and couldn't afford
to feed their horses anymore, her plans had changed.
She'd bought the horses for much more than they
were worth, helping her neighbor and giving the
horses a home. Thus, the barn became a stable.

Presley, an American quarter horse, extended
his graceful neck over the top of the stall door. He
snorted, his velvety muzzle snuffling against her shirt.

"Whoa there, boy. You know what I have for you,
don't you?" She pulled two sugar cubes from her
shirt pocket and placed them in the flat of her palm

so he wouldn't accidentally take a couple of fingers along with the treats. "Don't tell Piper I gave you sugar. She wouldn't approve."

Presley chomped loudly and was soon pushing against her shirt pocket again.

She crooned and rubbed his forehead. But when he realized she wasn't feeding him anything else, he turned his attention to the pail of oats Piper had hung earlier.

"Guess I know what's more important to you. Food trumps Emma every time."

"Not in my book."

She turned around at the sound of the deep voice. Six foot three inches of tantalizing male stood in the open doorway, his skin turning a deep gold as the setting sun's ray slanted across him. Macon's smile flashed as he started toward her. His ever-present shadow, Bogie, trotted beside him.

"Hope you don't mind me dropping in on my way home without calling first."

She cleared her throat and moved to the next stall. "Of course not. You said you'd try to check on me after work. You're always welcome here." Her Appaloosa was already straining his neck toward her, anxious for the same treats he saw Presley get. "I was hoping you'd be able to come earlier in the day, though, so we could have worked with Bogie. I'm guessing it was a bad scene this morning? The break-in?"

He stopped just past the first stall and leaned against it while she fed Elton his two sugar cubes.

"False alarm. Literally. A rat chewed through a wire and set off the security alarm."

"How do you know it was a rat?"

"I found the crispy critter with his teeth still gripping the wire."

"Aw. Poor guy."

"Poor guy? Your barn cat eats rats all the time, I'll bet."

"True. But that's nature, the circle of life. A rat getting electrocuted isn't a natural death."

He idly patted Bogie's head. "You won't find me shedding any tears over a rodent. But I get it. Life is precious. Any time it's wasted or cut short isn't something to celebrate." He motioned toward the Appaloosa. "Elton, right? And the other one is Presley?"

"You remembered."

"Hard to forget. Elton John. Elvis Presley. Two great rockers in their time. But I don't get where the name Gus came from for your barn cat." He motioned toward the orange cat just as he darted under one of the stall doors.

"Gus is short for Angus," she said. "Angus Young, guitarist for AC/DC."

He grinned, his sexy smile lighting up the barn far better than the overhead lights. "Gotta love consistency. I figure if I ever have another dog, I'll name it Bacall, to go along with Bogart."

"*Casablanca.* You could do worse."

"Actually it was Ingrid Bergman in *Casablanca.*"

She stopped petting Elton and stepped away from

the stall. "That's right. I'm so used to hearing Bogie
and Bacall, since they were in movies together and
got married. What if your next dog is a boy? What
would you name him?" She crouched down and gave
Bogie a command to come. He eagerly sat in front
of her, tail wagging, tongue lolling.

"Ernest, of course."

She blinked. "Ernest? Wait. Let me think." She
tapped her hands on her jeans. "Oh, of course. Bogie
and Bacall first met filming *To Have and Have Not*.
It was based on the novel by Ernest Hemingway."

"Bingo."

She laughed. "Your mind works in odd ways,
Macon."

"And yet your mind followed my line of reason-
ing. What does that say about you?" He winked and
she laughed again.

Presley chose that moment to put his head over
the half door and nudge against her pocket again. She
pushed his head away, stepping back. "No more sugar
cubes, boy. Not today."

He tossed his head and showed his displeasure by
kicking the back wall in his stall.

Bogie jerked hard against Macon, forcing him to
move away from the stall.

"Stop, Bogie. It's okay. There's nothing to be
afraid of." He knelt down and started petting the
shepherd, whispering soothing words. "This is what I
was telling you about," he told Emma. "Loud, sudden
noises scare him. He does this every time."

Emma crouched down in front of the shepherd. His eyes weren't wild. He wasn't shaking. But his fur was ruffled and he was staring at the stall door. She stood.

"Macon. He's not afraid. He's protecting you."

He gave her a doubtful look. "You think so? That's not how he's been trained to act when there's a threat. He's supposed to freeze in place, refuse to go forward. Or if there's an assailant, attack."

"Before the ambush, that's probably what he'd still do. But I've seen this kind of behavior before. He must be associating loud noises, like Presley kicking his stall, with the gunshot sounds when you and Ken were ambushed. So instead of going on the offensive, as he's supposed to do, he's being defensive. He's afraid, but not for himself. He's afraid for you."

He gently smoothed Bogie's fur. The shepherd had calmed now and sat down, panting happily as if nothing had happened.

"How do we fix him?" Macon asked.

She chuckled. "Fix him. Well, it's like we originally planned. He needs retraining. Not weeks or months like the last time. Well, maybe one week, or less if it goes well. Depends on how traumatized he is. I won't know until I work with him. Will you be able to bring him in tomorrow morning like we'd hoped to do today?"

"Possibly. Chief Walters has approved the training. But we're short on personnel right now with a couple of guys on vacation. So I still have to respond to calls when needed. Hard to predict. And I'm the lead investigating Angel, trying to find her family, and whether one of them or someone else left her at your doorstep. I'll bring him when I can but it might be spotty."

"I need to desensitize him. He needs to relearn that loud sounds aren't always bad and that you can handle yourself. One way to help him is to keep him on a regular routine. It will make him feel secure, that his environment is under control."

"If that's the case, then me not being able to commit to specific training times isn't doing him any favors."

"Exactly," she said. "How would you feel about dropping him off here in the mornings on your way to the police station? Then you can come train with him after your shifts are over and take him back home? It's imperative that he learn not to associate loud noises with you potentially dying, so he can stick to his training and go on the offensive and respond to your commands. To do that, I'll need you here during some of the training. But not the whole thing. We can compromise, have me work with him during the day and you come after work. I could throw in dinner afterward."

"Careful," he teased. "A home-cooked meal is a powerful bribe. And if it's even half as good as breakfast was this morning, you're in real trouble."

"I didn't say it would be home-cooked."

He smiled. "I should be able to come here most

late afternoons or evenings. Dropping him off on my way into town before work sounds good too. That'll fit in better around the meetings I get pulled into and shift turnover every morning."

"Good." She led the way toward the barn door. "We can start our new routine right now, with dinner."

After securing the barn door behind them, they started toward the house, Bogie trotting happily at Macon's side.

"Unfortunately, in spite of what I just said, I can't tonight. I've got an appointment. But when I had to leave so quickly this morning, I'd promised to stop back by. So I'm keeping that promise. I wanted to let you know I can't train today, and of course to apologize for not returning earlier."

"Did you? Apologize?" She glanced up at him, laughed at his startled expression. "Kidding. No apology needed or expected."

He put his hand on her shoulder, stopping her in front of the porch. "I am, you know. Sorry. I should have called."

She put her hands on her hips. "Cop's daughter, remember? Plus, my bonus dad is Chief Walters. I completely understand that you aren't a nine-to-five desk guy. I know the job's constraints, that you can't control your hours even when you try. So, seriously, no apologies."

"Understanding the job doesn't mean apologies aren't necessary. So I'll continue to apologize when warranted."

She shook her head. "Fine. Whatever makes you feel better. What's this appointment you're off to? Or is it confidential?"

"Not at all. I've been trying to get interviews lined up with those teens who help DCA out as part of their court-ordered community service. Not having much luck so far. Even their parents aren't responding to police calls asking for interviews. So I'm going to surprise them, try to catch them at home, starting with the Norvells, Kyle's parents."

"Can't you just wait and talk to them when they're working here one afternoon?"

"You told me Kyle and Hugh work Thursdays and Fridays. And William's days are irregular, whenever he can get here. I can't wait all week to talk to them. I have an investigation to run."

"So, what, you're just going to show up at Kyle's house tonight, alone? Dressed like that?"

He frowned and glanced down. "Something wrong with my uniform?"

"And your car. They both scream police."

He arched a brow. "That's kind of the idea of the uniform and marked car."

She waved her hand impatiently. "What I'm saying is that if your goal is to get Kyle, or his parents, to give you any information, you need to be more low-key. In their neighborhood, the police are the enemy. Parking a police car in their driveway and showing up at their door in uniform is going to do one thing—ensure they don't talk to you. You don't survive living in that kind of environment looking like a snitch who talks to the cops. Even if his parents aren't involved in any criminal activities, a lot of their neighbors likely are. They can't risk being seen talking to you."

"I *have* to talk to them. We're hunting down every lead we can to find Angel's family. You're the one who told me about Kyle, Hugh and William. I'd be negligent if I *don't* talk to them as part of this investigation. I have to rule them out, or in, as being involved."

Bogie whined, drawing their attention. His huge shepherd ears were perked up and his head was tilted at an adorable angle as he looked up at them.

Macon sighed and knelt down, rubbing Bogie's neck. "Sorry, boy. It's okay. We're not really arguing."

"Sure we are."

He gave her an aggravated look. "No. We're not."

She laughed.

His frown deepened.

She held out her hands in a placating gesture. "Truce, Lieutenant Ridley. Look, I'm not trying to be difficult. I'm actually trying to be helpful. I don't want you to drive to Kyle's home only to be turned away."

He patted Bogie again then stood. "I'm sensing a suggestion coming on."

"Then you have excellent instincts. My recommendation is that you go home and change into civilian clothes before heading over there. And you don't show up in a police car. What kind of personal car do you drive?"

"A black Ford pickup."

"Oh, good. That will fit right in. What year?"

"This year. I bought it before leaving Boise."

"It's brand-new?"

"That's what this year means."

"Okay, now you're starting to annoy me. Cut the sarcasm."

He drew a deep breath, then let it out slowly. "Sorry."

"Apology accepted."

"I thought you never wanted me to apologize."

"For being a cop. Not for being a jerk."

His mouth twitched as if he wanted to smile but he didn't. "Point taken. Unfortunately, the only vehicles I have right now are the police SUV and my, apparently, *too-new* shiny pickup."

"You have a third choice." She motioned behind him toward the parking spots to the left of the kennel building.

A pained expression crossed his face. "Instead of driving my new truck, you want me to drive that olive-green rust bucket of bolts?"

"That rusted bucket of bolts is a 1952 Chevy half-ton pickup with the original 235 straight six engine and wood deck in the back. It's an antique. A collector's item, a classic. It's museum-worthy."

"It belongs in a junkyard."

"It belonged to my father, Rick Daniels. And green was his favorite color."

"It's beautiful. Perfect. I'd be honored to drive it."

"Smart man. But you're not driving it."

He turned around. "Then why offer it?"

"I'll drive. I'm going with you."

"No. Absolutely not. Besides, you need to stay home to take care of Angel."

"I'll ask Barbara if she can stay late to take care of Angel until I get back. Think about it, Macon. I admit I haven't known Kyle and the other two teens very long. I haven't really established a rapport with them quite yet. But they're starting to trust me. And if the neighbors see me there, the Norvells can honestly tell them I'm in charge of their son's community service to keep him out of jail. They can say I stopped by to discuss his work and no one will worry that they were snitching on someone for, well, anything."

"Makes sense. I get it," he said. "But what if Kyle is the one behind abducting Angel or maybe she's his daughter and he abandoned her. Either way, he'd be worried about being arrested for his part in whatever is going on with her. It could be dangerous. You shouldn't be there."

"If that's your argument then Kyle shouldn't even be allowed at DCA."

"Maybe he shouldn't. I could talk to the judge about that."

"Don't you dare. These kids need this job to stay

out of jail and turn their lives around. If one of them is involved in what's going on with Angel, then they need our help more than ever. Besides, it's not like I'd be in that neighborhood, or in Kyle's home, by myself. You'd be with me. You'd protect me."

He shook his head. "No, Emma. You're not going with me. That's final."

Chapter Nine

Macon shook his head as Emma pulled her ancient pickup into the Norvells' driveway. "I can't believe I let you talk me into this."

"You're an intelligent man. You saw reason."

"I'm an idiot. I saw a beautiful woman and logic flew out the window."

She grinned. "Sweet of you to say that. Now let's go."

"Emma, I'm having second thoughts. I don't think this is a good—"

She jumped out of the truck and started toward the house.

Macon swore and hurried after her.

Once inside, Macon had to admit that Emma's strategy was correct. The Norvells admitted they wouldn't have opened the door except that Kyle recognized Emma. And while the parents weren't exactly warm and welcoming, they were civil and did seem to appreciate that Emma had agreed to let Kyle work at the Daniels Canine Academy as his required community service. Kyle, on the other hand, seemed indifferent and hadn't spoken more than to say hello since they'd come inside.

Since the teen seemed jumpy and anxious, and kept glancing at the front door as if he was going to make a run for it, Macon was glad he'd chosen a seat right beside the door. While Emma leaned forward in her chair making small talk with the parents on the couch, Macon kept his gaze trained on Kyle.

If Macon hadn't known the kid was seventeen, he'd have sworn he was in his early twenties. He was nearly as tall as Macon and had a world-weary look in his dark eyes whenever he actually made eye contact, which wasn't often. His hair looked as if it hadn't been washed in a few days and he kept shoving his too-long bangs back from his face.

The small home he and his family lived in spoke of a hard life without a lot of money. But it was neat and clean and showed pride in ownership. Everything seemed in good repair. Even the yard outside was well-maintained with some cheerful yellow flowers to the left and right of the front door.

While Kyle's parents' clothing looked worn and old, their son looked as if he'd just left a department store with brand-new sneakers, jeans and—surprisingly— a collared shirt. Macon had expected tattered jeans, holey shoes, and a T-shirt sporting some kind of profanity or reference to a heavy metal band. He'd based his expectations on the kid's rap sheet and mug shots. But maybe there was more to Kyle after all. Maybe he was struggling to make himself a life without the benefits of growing up in a family where money wasn't as hard to come by. And maybe he had nothing to do with Angel ending up on Emma's front porch. But if that was the case, why was he so nervous? And why did he look like he wanted to bolt?

"How do you like working at DCA, Kyle?" Macon asked.

Conversation on the other side of the room stopped and everyone looked at Macon. Except Kyle.

"Kyle," his father said, "answer the police officer."

Kyle frowned and crossed his arms, but he finally met Macon's gaze. "It's all right, I guess."

"Do you work with the dogs or the horses?"

"Not really. I mostly clean or make repairs." His gaze slid toward the door.

"Repairs," Macon said, trying to engage him in the conversation instead of hitting him up with hard questions he'd likely not answer. "I can see where there'd be a lot of things that need fixing on a spread of land like DCA. What kinds of things do you repair?"

He shrugged. "Fences. Doors. Siding. Junk like that."

"Siding. Like on the house?"

"The barn. It had some holes in it so Ms. Daniels asked me to replace some boards. No big deal. Dad, can I go now? You said I could hang out with my friends after dinner."

"That was before Officer Ridley showed up. Your friends can wait. Answer his questions."

Kyle sighed, his mouth tightening in a rebellious frown. "So ask me some questions, cop. Real questions. What do you want?"

"Kyle—"

"No, it's okay, Mr. Norvell," Macon told him. "Kyle has plans and I'm interfering. He's right. I should get to the point of my visit."

Instead of having built any trust or rapport in their short conversation, Macon could see Kyle tensing up in anticipation of whatever he was going to ask. Macon glanced at Emma, who was chewing her lip, but she only shrugged. She didn't have a long history with Kyle either, so they were both at a disadvantage.

"Do you have a girlfriend, Kyle?"

Kyle's eyes widened. Macon had definitely caught him off guard with that question.

"I, ah." The teen's gaze slid toward his parents before answering. "I got a few girls at school who like me. Nothing serious. What's that got to do with anything?"

"Did any of them have a baby about two months ago?"

Kyle's face reddened.

His father jumped to his feet. "What's going on here, Officer?"

Macon glanced at the father, but focused on Kyle as he answered. He didn't want to miss his reactions, verbal and nonverbal. "Last Saturday morning, someone left an approximately two-month-old baby girl on Ms. Daniels's front porch. We're trying to find out who the baby's parents are, and who left her at DCA."

"And you think that's me?" Kyle choked out, seemingly genuinely shocked.

Both of his parents were now standing and Emma was, too, speaking in low tones to Mrs. Norvell as if trying to soothe her anger. Before either of them could order him out of their house, Macon tried to lower the temperature in the room a few degrees.

"I have no idea who the baby's father is, or who left her there," Macon explained, keeping his voice calm. "But since you're at DCA several times a week, Ms. Daniels and I were hoping you could tell us if you've seen anyone suspicious lurking around. Or maybe while you've been out repairing fences, you've run across signs that someone's been watching the house. Footprints, broken branches in the shrubs near the house. That sort of thing. We're hoping you can help us. Even if you haven't seen signs of anyone else at the ranch, maybe you know about someone at school who had a baby recently and no one has seen the baby since."

Macon's little speech did what he'd hoped—it defused the situation. Mr. Norvell had stepped around the coffee table and was standing a few feet away now. But both he and Kyle seemed to have relaxed, if only a little. And it didn't seem as if the father was about to order Macon out of the house. Instead, he put his hand on his son's shoulder.

"Kyle, if you know anything, tell him. There's an innocent baby involved. He needs his family."

"She," Emma said, her voice quiet. She was holding Mrs. Norvell's hand as the two women watched them from across the room. "Her name is Angel. Or at least, that's what the note said that was left with her."

"She," Mr. Norvell corrected. "Kyle?"

Kyle held out his hands in a helpless gesture. "I don't know nothing. I swear. And I haven't seen anything to make me think someone was sneaking around DCA." He turned toward Emma. "I promise, Ms. Daniels. If I thought someone was trespassing, that you were in any danger, I'd tell you."

She smiled. "Thank you, Kyle. I appreciate that."

Something flickered in Kyle's expression. He was hiding something. The question was whether it had anything to do with Angel.

"What about your friends?" Macon asked. "William and Hugh. Do you think they could be involved?"

Kyle vigorously shook his head. "No way, man. You need to look at someone else."

"It's getting late, Officer Ridley." Mr. Norvell spoke in a hard tone, his meaning clear.

"Understood," Macon said. "I mean no offense to any of you. I have to follow up on all possible leads to get Angel, the baby, to her mom and dad."

This time it was Mrs. Norvell who spoke up. "Of course you do." She nodded at Emma, then went to stand beside her husband and son. "And if any of us hear anything that might help, we'll definitely let you know."

"That's all I can ask." Macon shook their hands as Emma joined him by the door. "Thank you for your time." He handed a business card to the father. "If you think of anything that might help with the case, please call me."

When they were in Emma's truck again and back on the road, she shook her head. "That went about as bad as it could have gone."

"I think it went just fine."

She shot him a startled look. "Fine? We didn't get any information."

"Sure we did. I didn't expect anyone to tell us much during this initial interview, not given their history with the police. The family is bound to circle the wagons, try to protect their son. But even if they didn't say much, their body language was loud and clear. The parents were shocked to hear about Angel. Based on that, I'm inclined to believe the baby's not Kyle's. It would be hard to imagine him having a pregnant girlfriend who gave birth two months ago without the Norvells knowing about it. They seem like involved parents. And Kyle treats them with respect, more or less. They're aware of what's going on in his life. I think they'd know about a baby."

"I didn't think of it that way, but you're probably right. What about Kyle? What did you pick up from him?"

"Kyle's not as easy to read. He seemed shocked,

too. But that might have been for his parents' ben-
efit. I got the impression he was hiding something."

"Like what? You just said you don't think he's the
father, that his parents would have known."

"It may not be related to the case. Maybe he's
done something else that he didn't want the cops to
know about. Or it could be something he's keeping
from his parents, unrelated to this investigation. Still,
I'm not convinced he doesn't know something about
Angel and who's responsible for abandoning her."

"Or kidnapping her."

"I'm really not leaning in that direction right now.
None of us working the case are. The parents would
have filed a missing persons report even if they were
leery of cops. I just can't see this as an abduction. I
think whoever left Angel was the mother or father."

"That's a relief, actually. I'd rather believe that the
person who trespassed on my property isn't some
hardened criminal stealing someone's child."

"Don't get me wrong. We're looking at every possibility, keeping an open mind. I'm just saying that
right now, it seems more likely that one of Angel's
parents left her on your porch."

"I get it. And I appreciate that you're not jumping
to conclusions. It's important to know exactly what's
going on and why."

"Turn down that next road coming up."

She glanced toward where he was pointing. "That
won't take us back to DCA."

"No. It won't." He glanced at the screen on his

phone. "In spite of Mr. Norvell proclaiming that it was getting late, it's only going on eight o'clock. Hugh Engel's home isn't far from here, down that road. How do you feel about doing one more interview tonight?"

In answer, she slowed and made the requested turn. "If it helps with the investigation, I'm all for it. I've spoken to Hugh's parents before but it was at DCA. I've never been to his house. Give me the address and then you can call Barbara to make sure everything's okay with the baby."

"On it."

While Hugh wasn't home because he was out somewhere with his father, his mother was. And she didn't have the same reservations about talking to a police officer that the Norvells had. She readily answered every question that Macon asked. And she promised him that she'd check with other parents at the school to see if anyone had a baby in the past couple of months. She told Macon to expect a call tomorrow with the results of her inquiries. And she also said she'd have Hugh call him and arrange a meeting.

"That was refreshing," Emma said, when they were in her truck again, driving down the highway.

"Agreed. It's nice to question someone who doesn't seem to be hiding anything. Hopefully I'll get the same kind of cooperation from Hugh himself once I speak with him. Now for William Shrader." He checked the time on his phone again. "It really is getting late. I may have to try to interview him tomorrow. Let me look up his address and see how far away he lives."

"No need." Emma slowed and turned into a long driveway much like her own. "I've been here before. That SUV in front of the house belongs to William's dad. And that—" she pointed toward the right side of the long ranch home where a light shone in a window "—is William's room. He's home."

Chapter Ten

Emma shifted her weight in her kitchen chair, trying to ease the ache in her arms from holding the sleeping baby. She glanced at Macon, who was loading the dishwasher a few feet away, just as he'd done Tuesday and Wednesday after she'd fixed them dinner. The week was flying by.

She enjoyed seeing him each night, and during the day when he was able to fit in some training time with Bogie. But she was becoming increasingly frustrated that he was being so vague about the investigation, especially about what was going on with Kyle, William, and Hugh.

Back on Monday night, when she and Macon had stopped at William's home, it hadn't turned out as she'd expected. His parents claimed he wasn't there, in spite of the light in his window. And they hadn't even invited Macon and Emma inside.

Macon had reminded her that he couldn't force the parents to let him check William's bedroom without a warrant. Given Emma's own teenaged experiences on the wrong side of law enforcement, she'd known that. But she hadn't expected the family to refuse them entry. She'd thought her earlier meetings with them and reassurances that she wanted to help their son would have made a difference. Her being with Macon should have, in theory, eased their fears and made them want to cooperate. It hadn't.

When Macon finished putting the dirty dishes in the dishwasher and turned it on, she shifted in her chair again. Now, maybe she could finally get that update.

"Careful," she teased. "I could get used to having a man clean my kitchen every night."

He dried his hands on the dish towel hanging from her oven door and turned around, bracing his hands against the counter on either side of him as he stretched out his long legs. "It's the least I can do when you're the one providing the food." He nodded toward Bogie, who was resting by the back kitchen door. "To both of us. I may stop soon anyway if you continue to refuse to let me pay you."

"Sharing with Bogie isn't a burden. I buy dog food in bulk at Sampson's Feed and Grain just outside of town. Plus, Jasper PD is compensating me for training him. As for feeding you, I've never learned how to make dinner just for one. And I enjoy having you here."

Her face flushed warm at that admission, especially since his eyes widened slightly. He had to know she was wildly attracted to him, since she'd made no secret about that when they'd first met. And she was confident he felt the same way about her. They'd fallen back into their easy banter as if he hadn't been living in Boise for the past two years, as if he'd never left. But that didn't mean she wanted things to go further. She had to guard her heart against getting hurt.

It wasn't that he had a girlfriend. She'd nonchalantly worked that question into one of their conversations and knew he wasn't currently seeing anyone. The problem was her fear that she could fall for him and then he'd decide to move back to Boise.

His very large extended family was there. It made sense he'd probably want to return, once he healed more from the loss of his friend and survivor's guilt. She didn't want to be a fling in his memories or be left pining over him. No, it was better if she was careful. Encouraging a relationship beyond their easy friendship wasn't fair to either of them.

She cleared her throat. "Bogie is doing much better already. I don't think his trauma was nearly as bad as we both initially thought."

His warm brown eyes flickered toward the dog again, who was now lightly snoring. "I was thinking the same thing. This afternoon's session went really well. It's a relief to know he hasn't been scarred for life."

"Unlike you?" she asked softly.

He winced. "Maybe. But I can handle it. If losing one of my best friends *didn't* affect me, I'd be a cold loser."

"Well, you definitely aren't that."

Angel smacked her lips and burrowed her head deeper into the blanket covering her.

Macon sidled over and smiled down at the sleeping baby. "I swear she's grown already since I first saw her."

"You're probably right. I'm just relieved she's so healthy." She sighed wistfully. "It's hard to remember sometimes that she's not mine. She belongs to someone else. We need to find her family."

"Before you become too attached?"

"Something like that." She swallowed at the lump in her throat. "How are your inquiries going? Did you ever speak to William? Did Hugh's mom have him call you? I know you don't want to share every detail of an ongoing case. But this one directly impacts me. And I'm working with those kids. They were all here today. It was kind of awkward not knowing what's going on where they're concerned."

He hesitated, as if trying to figure out how to phrase his answer. Then he shrugged. "I suppose that's fair. Hugh's mom finally called me back and provided an alibi for him for when Angel was left here. She provided pictures from a fishing trip he and his dad went on the weekend she was abandoned. They left Friday after school and didn't get back until Sunday night. We pulled cell phone records to verify it, and corroborated her claims with other witnesses. Hugh was definitely at a lake several hours away."

"That's good to know. And William? Did you speak to him yet?"

He nodded. "Several times, actually. Including earlier today. You were out in the field with Piper and the horses when I arrived. The boys were taking a break outside the kennel building. Honestly, I feel like none of them are very forthcoming. It could be their overall distrust of cops. But with Kyle, in particular, it seems as if he's hiding something. What I need to know is whether that has anything to do with Angel. All three of the boys claim they don't know anyone who's had a baby recently."

"Maybe they're telling the truth."

"Maybe. But I'm not letting them off the hook that easily. Kyle and the others seem really tight. I can't imagine that one of them is involved in this and the others don't know about it. The trick is in getting someone to crack."

She shifted her arm again. "I think you should leave them alone and explore other leads."

"It seems as if she gets heavier the longer you hold her, doesn't it? Let me take her and give you a break."

Before she could think of a reason to say no, he gently lifted Angel out of her arms and cuddled her against his chest. There was an ache in her own chest as she watched him smiling down at the baby. And she couldn't honestly say it was just because she selfishly wanted to hold Angel herself.

A full minute passed and the baby didn't so much as gurgle. Emma shook her head in wonder. "That wasn't fair. You distracted me to get me to stop asking questions."

He grinned, but didn't deny it.

She laughed and decided to let it drop. "She sure is comfortable with you. Piper can't even pick her up without Angel crying. Only Barbara and I can hold her and keep her happy, or so I thought."

"Maybe she still thinks you're holding her. She's asleep, after all."

"Trust me. It's something about you that makes her feel safe. I've tried transferring her to Piper while Angel was sleeping. And once to the veterinarian technician, Tashya, when she stopped by to vaccinate some of the dogs. As soon as she left my arms she jerked awake and started bawling. It didn't matter what Piper or Tashya said or tried. You really do have the magic touch. You'd be a good father."

His warm gaze flew to hers. "Thank you. You'd be a great mother, obviously."

She immediately shook her head. "No. No, I wouldn't. I'm not having children. Ever."

He frowned and looked like he wanted to argue with her, so she quickly slid her chair back. "I need to put her down for the night and shower and hit the hay soon myself. The dogs will be howling for breakfast if I oversleep."

"I thought Piper feeds them for you."

"Actually, Barbara used to do that and Piper mainly helped with the training. But with Angel being here, we've juggled the chores around. Piper and I clean, feed and train together while Barbara stays in the house with the baby and takes care of the administrative tasks for running this place. Regardless, the point is I help in the mornings, no matter who's feeding them. It's a big job."

She reached for the baby, and he seemed to reluctantly pass her back. After adjusting the blanket around the baby to make sure she was warm, Emma smiled up at Macon. "Thank you again, for everything. We're making great progress with Bogie. And hopefully the investigation will be resolved soon and we can all get back to our normal lives."

He stared at her a long moment, his gaze intense, questioning. "Is that what you want? For both of us to return to our normal lives, the way they were before Angel came along?"

Her chest tightened uncomfortably, well aware of what he really meant. He was asking about the possibility of them continuing their friendship and seeing where it might lead. But she wasn't ready for that, didn't think she'd ever be ready. And since she didn't even fully understand it herself, she didn't want to get into a discussion about it. So instead, she did what she'd always done when anyone got too close. She shut him down.

"Yes. I'm sure. I don't have time for a baby, not really. Or anything else right now. I'm too busy."

He stared at her until her face began to grow warm beneath the lie. Then he gave her a crisp nod. "Understood. Bogie, come on, boy."

The shepherd's ears perked up as he blinked his sleepy eyes.

Macon patted his thigh. "Come on. Home."

The word *home* had the shepherd eagerly rising to his feet, tail wagging, tongue lolling out. He trotted to Macon and looked up at him adoringly.

Emma followed the two of them to the front door.

Once on the porch, Macon paused as if to say something else, but seemed to think better of it. Instead, he jogged down the steps to his SUV.

Chapter Eleven

Emma jerked awake, bolting upright in her bed and covering her ears against the shrill, pulsating sound of her house's security alarm going off. The kennels erupted into frantic barking as the dogs reacted to the noise. Groggy and confused, she scanned her bedroom. It was pitch-dark, still nighttime. What was going on? Was the alarm malfunctioning? Or was someone trying to break in? Maybe they already had. A cold sweat broke out on her forehead in spite of the coolness of the house.

Desperate cries sounded from the guest room next door. *Angel!* Emma jumped out of bed and grabbed her Glock from the nightstand drawer. Her cell phone started ringing on top of the nightstand. She swiped it as she sprinted out of the bedroom and into Angel's room.

After slamming the door shut and locking it, she glanced at the screen, ready to send the call to voice mail so she could dial 911. But caller ID showed it was the alarm company. She put the phone on speaker mode and then pressed the screen to accept the call, before setting the phone on top of the chest of drawers so she could check on the baby.

"Ms. Daniels, this is—"

"The alarm company. I know. Please get the police out here. I think someone is either trying to break into my house or is already inside. Tell the police that I'm locked in the baby's bedroom with her, front right corner of the house. And I've got a pistol. So they'd better announce themselves when they get here."

She leaned over the crib, her heart squeezing in her chest at the sight of Angel's red face and the tears tracking down her little cheeks. But she didn't dare pick her up yet. She trained her pistol on the bedroom door, ready to go down shooting if someone busted inside. She had to protect the baby.

"Ms. Daniels, I've notified Jasper PD. Please stay on the line while—"

"Sorry. Can't." She ended the call and pressed the favorites button on her phone. Then she hit the very first number.

The call picked up before the second ring. "Emma, what's wrong?"

Relief flooded through her. "Macon, the alarm—"

"Is going off. I hear it. I'll be there in two minutes." She could hear sounds, the rustling of fabric, keys jangling. "Where are you?"

"In the front bedroom, Angel's room. It's the last door down the hall on the right side."

"And the baby?"

"With me. The door's locked. I've got my pistol."

"Good." He sounded relieved. An engine roared to life. "Don't open that door to anyone but me."

"I'll need to let you in the front—"

"No. Stay in the bedroom until I get there."

She put the phone on speaker again and set it on top of the chest of drawers, keeping her pistol trained on the bedroom door the whole time. She couldn't hear Macon anymore if he was talking to her. But she had to focus, concentrate. The chaotic blaring of the alarm, the dogs barking and Angel screaming, along with the fear that someone was in the house, that they might try to break through the door at any second, had her shaking so hard she could barely hold the gun up.

"It's okay, baby girl," she called out toward the crib, her gaze glued on the door. "I'm so sorry I can't pick you up yet. This will all be over soon. Shh, shh, shh."

Bam! A door banged somewhere in the house.

She jumped at the new sound. Had Macon arrived? Had he busted down the front door to get to her? Or was someone else inside?

The pistol slipped. She grabbed it before it could fall and wrapped both hands around the grip, struggling to stop shaking. But even her teeth were chattering.

Another sound intruded between the ear-splitting pulses of the alarm. Footsteps. In the hallway.

Emma tensed, her finger tightening against the frame of the gun. She knew not to put it on the trigger until she was ready to fire. Her daddy had taught her that.

"Emma, it's Macon. I'm in the hallway. Are you okay?"

Relief nearly made her slump to the floor. "Yes. Yes, we're okay."

"The house is clear. Bogie's on guard in the main room. No one's getting past him. What's your alarm code?"

She told him, and moments later the sound blessedly stopped. The sudden quiet must have startled Angel, because she quit crying.

"You can open the door now," Macon called out.

Emma set the pistol down and ran to the door. Her hands were still shaking so much it took two tries to unlock it. Then she flung it open and was immediately wrapped in Macon's arms. She didn't resist his tight hug. Instead, she reveled in it as he backed her into the room.

The sound of the door closing, then locking, had her stiffening against him.

"It's okay," he soothed. "I didn't see any intruders, but the back door had been jimmied open. That's how I got in. I'm guessing they didn't actually come inside because the alarm scared them away. But I'm not taking any chances that they're still on the property. We'll stay right here until more police arrive. I radioed them on my way here."

"Th-the…alarm…company called 911 t-too."

He gently pushed her back and held on to her

shoulders. His brow furrowed with concern. "Are you sure you're okay?"

She laughed, or would have except her throat was so dry it came out as a raspy croak. She cleared her throat and tried again. "I'm fine. I really am. Thanks to you."

He gently squeezed her arms. "And the baby?"

She blinked. "Oh my gosh." About the time she spoke, Angel started screaming again. "Angel, poor baby. It's okay." She ran to the crib and scooped her up in her arms, rocking her against her chest. "It's okay, sweet girl. It's okay. Don't cry. Shh, shh, shh."

MACON NODDED AT what Chief Walters was telling him. But when Captain Rutledge interrupted to say something derogatory about DCA, Macon stepped away. Why Rutledge had even shown up was a mystery. He certainly wasn't contributing anything helpful to the situation. And he hadn't even bothered to ask whether Emma was okay, as pretty much every other officer on the scene had done.

Macon stopped near the end of the couch so he could see Emma through the kitchen opening. Still cradling Angel, she was sitting at the table listening to Piper and Barbara, who were sitting beside her. They'd both arrived shortly after dawn to begin their usual work routine and had been shocked to see all the police cars lining the driveway. Half of Jasper PD had shown up to make sure that Emma was safe.

And Bogie wouldn't leave her side. He was curled up at her feet beneath the table.

"She's tougher than you think," Walters assured him, straightening the hat he always wore, even inside, thinking no one would realize he was going bald. "Emma will be fine."

"Tough or not, she's exhausted. We need to wrap this up."

Rutledge asked the chief a question, drawing his attention.

Cal Hoover stepped through the front door with his rookie-in-training, Jason, at his side. He glanced at the chief, but Walters pointed at Macon and went back to his conversation with Rutledge.

Hoover stopped in front of Macon and handed him a set of keys. "I've sent the team back to the station. We've collected all the evidence we could find. Nothing else we can do here. The inside of the RV doesn't look like it's been touched in weeks, maybe longer. There weren't any prints on the outside, either. This whole place is pristine. Even the kennels didn't yield many prints. We dusted the gates, doorways, the faucets on the sinks in both the kennels and the barn. Got a few prints, not many. But I'm betting those belong to the staff, not our perpetrator. Because whoever started to break in through the back door didn't leave any prints."

"He wore gloves."

"That's my guess. He did leave a few shoeprints, a trail, more or less. It starts by the front porch, which means he probably stuck to the gravel prior to that or I'd have found some more prints out front in the grass. Then he left a few shoeprints around the side of the house, and at the bottom of the deck. Well, assuming they don't turn out to belong to anyone who works here."

Macon stared at him. "By the front porch? Someone hid behind the shrubs? Again?"

"Yep."

"Those dang things need to be chopped down. They're like a welcome sign to a wanna-be intruder." Macon scratched the stubble along his jaw. "None of this makes sense. Someone goes to the trouble of wearing gloves but is careless enough to leave shoeprints. And he doesn't case the place before trying to break in or he'd have known there was a security alarm. What does that sound like to you?"

"A budding criminal who isn't very smart?"

"Or a budding criminal who isn't very experienced. Yet." Visions of the three teens—Kyle, William and Hugh—danced in Macon's head. Every time he told himself they weren't involved in what was going on at DCA, something else happened to keep them on his persons of interest list. "What I don't get is why. If it's to rob the place, why try breaking in when Emma's truck is here? Everyone in town knows about DCA, that Emma lives out here, alone. Why not wait until she goes into town on a weekend, when Piper and Barbara aren't around, and rob it then?" Macon's blood ran cold as the answer came to him. And from the worried expression on Cal's face, he'd come to the same conclusion.

"The bastard knew Emma was alone this time of night, or this time of morning, I guess." Macon fisted his hands beside him. "He wasn't here to rob. He was here for Emma. Or Angel."

Cal cursed beneath his breath and glanced toward the kitchen. He moved closer, keeping his voice low. "I'm right with you on that train of thought. It's too big a coincidence that someone trespasses and drops off a kid. Then someone else trespasses trying to break in a handful of days later."

"We may have two perpetrators," Macon said. "Someone wanting to get rid of a baby, and someone else wanting her back?"

"Could be," Cal agreed.

"The question is, are they both bad guys, or is one a good guy? If it was Angel's mother who left her here, maybe she was trying to protect her from someone else. And that someone else has figured out where she left the baby."

"Another twist on that," Cal took up the theory, "could be that the person who tried to break in tonight was either trying to *save* the baby—"

"Or *kill* her."

Cal grimaced. "This is bad. Really bad. And getting more complicated by the minute." He motioned to Jason behind him. "Recall the team. I want to go over this place again. Look for more evidence. There has to be something we've missed." He put his hand on Macon's shoulder as Jason hurried out the front door. "We'll figure it out. We'll get this guy." He shook his head. "Or both of them."

When Cal headed outside, Macon updated the chief and the captain. They discussed strategies and where the investigation was going. They left shortly after that to return to the station, while Macon stayed behind.

He glanced toward the kitchen again. Piper was holding Angel while Barbara stood at the stove, stirring something in a frying pan. It appeared that she was making Emma breakfast. She was in good hands for now. Which meant Macon could do what he'd been wanting to do ever since he got here.

Confront Kyle and his friends.

If they didn't have alibis for early this morning, he was going to personally drag them into the station to answer his questions. Either they were involved, or they weren't. But he dang well wanted to know which way to go with that so he could stop wasting time on them if they were innocent and had no helpful information.

A few hours later, Macon turned his truck up Emma's now-empty driveway, disappointed to see that everyone from Jasper PD was gone. Piper's and Barbara's vehicles were still parked beside Emma's truck, so at least she wasn't alone. But he didn't like not having an officer stationed at her home with what had happened in the early hours before sunrise. Thankfully Bogie was here since Macon had left him to guard her before leaving earlier. But still, one of his fellow officers should have stuck around, per his discussion with Chief Walters.

He jogged up the front steps, barely pausing long enough to rap on the door before opening it.

Emma stopped in the middle of the family room, a thick stack of papers clutched in one hand and a smile on her face. "Macon, hi. I didn't realize you were coming back. I figured you'd wrap up things this morning at the station and then go home to catch up on your sleep. That's what I'm going to do as soon as I finish reviewing some paperwork Barbara needs me to sign."

"I have a few things to take care of, too, before I can take a nap. Where's Bogie?"

"At the kennels, for training. Piper and I talked about how I've been working with him. She's taking over for the morning."

"And Barbara?" He glanced around. "Where is she?"

"Well, ah, she's in the office in the kennel building, with Angel. She knew I was tired and she didn't want Angel to cry and wake me up once I lie down. Otherwise she'd be in my office here." She frowned. "Is something wrong?"

"Other than the fact that someone tried to break into your home early this morning? And I can't find your community-service kids to check their alibis? And you're in this house, alone, without anyone to protect you?"

"Hold it. Stop. Back up. *Community-service kids?* You mean Kyle, William and Hugh? You think one of them is responsible for the break-in?"

"Maybe. Maybe not. But I sure would like to ask them about it. Funny thing is, no one seems to know where they are, even though it's a school day."

"O…kay. Well, Kyle and Hugh should be here this afternoon. You could try talking to them then."

"I plan on it. That doesn't resolve the problem of you being here alone."

"Oh, for Pete's sake. I'm not alone. Piper's here. Barbara's here. Kyle and Hugh, possibly William too, will be here later—"

"Which is exactly why you shouldn't be here without protection. One or all of those kids could be involved in what's going on."

She tossed her stack of papers on one of the end tables and put her hands on her hips. "And what exactly *is* going on, Macon? Does anyone know? Because I sure don't. What's happening with the investigation about Angel? Do you have any leads aside from your police bias against troubled youths, jumping to conclusions and always assuming they're behind anything bad that happens? Even though you supposedly cleared Hugh earlier?"

He stiffened. "Police bias? You think that, what, I'm harassing Kyle and the others? For no reason?"

She crossed her arms. "Are you? I'm struggling to build trust with them, to help them turn their lives around. And they see me working every day with the police officer who keeps showing up at their houses and throwing accusations at them. Don't you have any adults to interview for this case? It can't be that hard to figure out who gave birth to a baby girl two months ago and suddenly doesn't have the child with them anymore. Who are Angel's parents? Are you *ever* going to find out? Are you even trying?"

The sound of someone clearing their throat had Macon slowly turning around. Cal stood in the door-way, his troubled gaze flickering back and forth between them.

"Hey," Cal said, his expression smoothing into a smile. "The door was open. Macon, what's with the saws, pruning shears and garbage bags in the back of your pickup? You here to attack the shrubs like you threatened earlier this morning?"

Macon cleared his throat, taking a moment before he trusted himself to speak. "If Emma approves it, yes."

Emma stepped forward as Cal joined Macon. Her face was a light red, which could mean she was either still angry or embarrassed. Macon didn't even try to figure out which one. He was too angry to care.

"Hi, Cal." She looked at Macon. "Attack my shrubs?"

He drew a calming breath. Then two, before speaking again. "The perpetrator this morning hid behind them in almost the same place as the person who hid there before abandoning Angel. I want to prune them low to the ground so no one can hide anymore.

If you give me your permission. It won't hurt them. They'll grow back. But I obviously recommend you keep them trimmed low in the future."

"I, ah, okay."

Macon gave her a curt nod and faced Cal. "Are you here for the security detail?"

"Security detail?" Emma echoed. "What are you talking about? Macon? Cal?"

Cal glanced at Macon as if for permission. Macon was too disgusted and tired to do more than nod.

"Two 911 calls out here in less than a week is troubling," Cal told Emma. "Especially since someone actually tried to break into your home. Macon asked the chief to post someone here when he's not around. Having a police car out front is a good deterrent. And having an officer here just in case something else happens will make all of us feel better. Things got a little mixed up in the chaos earlier and we all bugged out at the same time. I'm back to watch out for you until Jason arrives. He volunteered to take first shift."

"Oh. Well, thank you. That does ease my mind. I appreciate it. And thank you, Macon, for setting it up."

"I have some bushes to trim." He strode out of the house.

EMMA STARED AT the now-empty doorway Macon had just gone through, her face turning hot as she faced Cal. She offered him a wobbly smile. "Sorry you walked in during my tirade. I'm way too tired to be thinking straight, obviously. I never intended to say any of that out loud. But I'm so frustrated that Macon's investigation seems to be focused entirely on the teens helping me out around here. I wish he'd focus on someone else."

Cal squeezed her shoulder, then dropped his hand. "You've known me for years, Emma. You know how we police work, from watching your dad, then Walters when he took you under his wing and helped you avoid juvie."

She didn't think her face could get any hotter. "I'd rather forget my rebellious criminal days."

"I'm sure you would. And I'm not trying to throw that in your face. I'm just pointing out that you have the background, on both sides of this. You know how investigations work, that most of what the police do is kept close to the vest. On the surface, it may seem like not much is being done. But under the water, we're paddling like crazy."

She nodded. "I shouldn't have gone off on him like that. I'm aggravated, and tired."

"We all are. Macon more than the rest of us. He's barely had any sleep since this whole thing started. He's convinced the chief to let everyone, and I mean everyone, work this thing as time permits, in between other cases going on. But, Emma, it's not just about those three kids you're so protective of. Macon's doing due diligence with them, looking into potential alibis. It would be negligent not to. They have criminal records. They're here a lot so they know the place, where to hide, when you're alone. They may resent you because they're forced to work here by the court. But that's only a small fraction of what he's been looking into, what he's got all of us looking into."

She shifted on her feet, guilt weighing heavily as Cal continued.

"We have a status meeting every morning at the station, so believe me, I know what all is being done. And it's a lot. We've interviewed dozens of people so far and that number goes up every day. We're coordinating with other counties, the hospitals, to find Angel's mother. You can't just call up an administrator and say, hey, give me the names of all the women who had a baby there in the past few months. We have to work with judges to force them to do it. That's not easy when we don't have anything pointing to a specific person as a suspect. We're looking for similar crimes, anyone who's gotten out of jail recently who might be in the area causing trouble. We're investigating you too."

"Wait, me? What do you mean? Why?"

"Angel, her being left here. It could be random, but it could be personal, someone who knows you. We're looking at everyone who was fostered here, their families, their friends. That's not easy either. People scatter, get married, change names, move away. It's not like on TV where you press a magic button on a computer and someone's entire life history pops up on a screen. We have to dig, pound the pavement, go all over the county, neighboring counties, talking to anyone who will listen to us. Every time we do hit on potential suspects, and we have, it's a tedious, huge amount of work to rule them out, or keep looking at them. It all takes time. But trust me, Emma. We're putting in the hours, doing the work. We're following every bread crumb. Macon's not stopping until we resolve this thing. He's going to make sure you're safe and he's going to do it by following every lead, even when it means questioning some troubled teens. He'll figure this out. But it's not going to happen overnight."

She slowly sank onto the couch and wrapped her arms around her middle. "If you're trying to make me feel miserable, you've succeeded."

He sighed and sat beside her. "Emma, I'm not trying to make you feel bad. I just wanted you to know the truth. Macon's not the type to praise himself or expound on all the hard work he's doing, and that he's got us doing, on your behalf. He's working harder on this than anyone. And he doesn't deserve to be accused of basically being lazy and conducting a shoddy investigation."

She winced and drew a shaky breath. "I screwed up. I really screwed up."

He took her hand in his. "You reacted to a stressful situation with very little information to go on, with only a few hours of sleep. It's entirely understandable. But now you know the truth." He squeezed her hand and let it go. "I'm going outside to see what's taking Jason so long to get here. In the meantime, think about taking a nap. I can see how tired you are. You don't have to worry about being safe. We've got this."

"I know you do. I know Macon does." She cleared her throat. "Thanks, Cal."

He smiled, then headed outside.

A few moments later, Emma crossed to the front windows. Cal was standing by his police SUV in the circular driveway talking on his cell phone, presumably to Jason. Macon was tossing several full garbage bags into the back of his black pickup truck. It was a surprisingly large pile of bags for the short amount of time that he'd been outside. But watching him return to the line of shrubs along the front foundation, she could see how he'd filled those bags so fast. He whacked at the bushes quickly and efficiently, as if he was in a hurry and couldn't wait to leave.

Because of her.

"I really messed up," she whispered, hating herself in that moment. Here was a man who'd suffered a terrible loss, the death of his best friend. And he'd nearly been killed himself. Then he'd come here, looking to start a new, quieter life. But that didn't happen. Instead, he was doing everything he could to help her, to make her safe, to make her life better. And she'd paid him back by doubting him, questioning him, forgetting everything she knew about police work. He didn't deserve to be treated that way, especially by someone who knew him as well as she did. She knew the kind of person he was, knew he wasn't the type to look for the easy way out. He was exactly what Cal had portrayed, a driven detective who wouldn't stop until he solved this case and made sure Emma was okay.

She pressed a hand against the window as Macon bent to yank out some of the branches he'd just cut. She needed to apologize. But how? She'd been awful. She watched him for several minutes as he loaded more bags into the back of the truck. In spite of the mild temperatures outside, he was sweating, which was understandable given the hard work he was doing. He paused to wipe his forehead before turning back to the last shrub. A drink. He needed a cold drink. Not sure whether he preferred pop or iced tea, she took a gamble and decided he'd want tea. She'd have to make a fresh pitcher.

A few minutes later, she stepped onto the porch with a large glass of iced tea in her hand. But the smile she had for Macon died as she watched his truck turning out of the driveway onto the road out front.

Chapter Twelve

"She really is a good baby." Emma raised the side rail on the crib. It had been a long day for all of them, especially Angel, having been jolted awake by the shrill blaring of the house alarm. But in spite of that, and so many people in and out of the house all day, she'd settled down for the night with almost no fuss.

"The best." Barbara leaned past Emma and adjusted the blanket. "I can't help thinking about her mom. That's who you think left her, right?"

"Seems to make the most sense. The police are keeping an open mind on that point, but they're leaning toward it being the mother. Macon said as much the last time we spoke about it." She fisted her hands, wondering when she'd speak to him again. After he'd chopped up her shrubs and left this morning, he hadn't even called to check on her. Before she'd been so horrible to him, he'd definitely have called.

Barbara nodded. "Even if she left her because she felt forced to, to protect her somehow, she still has to be missing her, wondering how she's doing."

Emma led the way out of the room, back into the family room before replying. "I've thought about this so many times, doubting that a mother would leave her child in that way. But it just doesn't make sense to me that it would be anyone else who did it. Because if the mother doesn't know where her child is, she'd have been calling 911, the media, going door to door in her neighborhood to spread the word that her baby was missing. We'd have heard something."

"Agreed. Angel must have been abandoned by her mother."

"Or the father." Officer Jason Wright, who'd been assigned guard duty this afternoon, stepped inside with Bogie at his heels. The shepherd instantly went to Emma, as was his habit now, and lay down on the floor beside her. "Just did my rounds. Nothing to report. Everything looks okay."

"Thanks, Jason." Emma bent down to pet Bogie before standing again. "And you're right. It could be the father, too. But I still think the mom has to know, or it would have been reported."

"What if there is no mother?" Jason asked. "Maybe something happened to her. A car accident or something like that. And the dad can't handle a baby on his own. Maybe he heard about DCA, knows you've fostered before, and thought she'd have better care if left with you than left at the door of a fire station or hospital. Macon's gone over those possibilities and more with us. It's all part of the different theories we're pursuing."

FREE BOOK GIVEAWAY

2 FREE SUSPENSE BOOKS!

2 FREE SUSPENSEFUL ROMANCE BOOKS!

GET UP TO FOUR FREE BOOKS & TWO FREE GIFTS WORTH OVER $20!

We pay for everything!

See Details Inside

Dear Reader,

I am writing to announce the launch of a huge **FREE BOOKS GIVEAWAY**... and to let you know that YOU are entitled to choose up to FOUR fantastic books that WE pay for.

Try **Harlequin® Romantic Suspense** books featuring heart-racing page-turners with unexpected plot twists and irresistible chemistry that will keep you guessing to the very end.

Try **Harlequin Intrigue® Larger-Print** books featuring action-packed stories that will keep you on the edge of your seat. Solve the crime and deliver justice at all costs.

Or **TRY BOTH!**

In return, we ask just one favor: Would you please participate in our brief Reader Survey? We'd love to hear from you.

This FREE BOOKS GIVEAWAY means that your introductory shipment is completely free, <u>even the shipping</u>! If you decide to continue, you can look forward to curated monthly shipments of brand-new books from your selected series, always at a discount off the cover price! <u>Plus you can cancel any time</u>. Who could pass up a deal like that?

Sincerely

Pam Powers

Pam Powers
For Harlequin Reader Service

Complete the survey below and return it today to receive up to 4 FREE BOOKS and FREE GIFTS guaranteed!

FREE BOOKS GIVEAWAY
Reader Survey

1
Do you prefer stories with suspenseful storylines?

◯ YES ◯ NO

2
Do you share your favorite books with friends?

◯ YES ◯ NO

3
Do you often choose to read instead of watching TV?

◯ YES ◯ NO

YES! Please send me my Free Rewards, consisting of **2 Free Books** from each series I select and **Free Mystery Gifts**. I understand that I am under no obligation to buy anything, no purchase necessary see terms and conditions for details.

❏ **Harlequin® Romantic Suspense** (240/340 HDL GRNT)
❏ **Harlequin Intrigue® Larger-Print** (199/399 HDL GRNT)
❏ **Try Both** (240/340 & 199/399 HDL GRN5)

FIRST NAME | LAST NAME

ADDRESS

APT.# | CITY

STATE/PROV. | ZIP/POSTAL CODE

EMAIL ❏ Please check this box if you would like to receive newsletters and promotional emails from Harlequin Enterprises ULC and its affiliates. You can unsubscribe anytime.

Your Privacy – Your information is being collected by Harlequin Enterprises ULC, operating as Harlequin Reader Service. For a complete summary of the information we collect, how we use this information and to whom it is disclosed, please visit our privacy notice located at https://corporate.harlequin.com/privacy-notice. From time to time we may also exchange your personal information with reputable third parties. If you wish to opt out of this sharing of your personal information, please visit www.readerservice.com/consumerschoice or call 1-800-873-8635. **Notice to California Residents** – Under California law, you have specific rights to control and access your data. For more information on these rights and how to exercise them, visit https://corporate.harlequin.com/california-privacy.

HI/HRS-122-FBG22_HI/HRS-122-FBGVR

"I'm not surprised." Barbara grabbed her purse from the decorative table near the front door. "He seems to be on top of things from what I've seen. He'll get this figured out soon enough. You need anything, Emma, give me a call. I'm not far away."

"I think we'll be fine. But I really appreciate it, Barb. Thanks for everything."

Barbara waved her fingers and headed outside.

"Piper left a few minutes ago," Jason announced. "She wanted me to let you know that Shane called, said their new corgi-pit puppy, Chipper, wasn't doing too well. They're taking him to the vet."

The guilt that had been churning inside Emma again over how she'd treated Macon took a back seat to the worry that now flared with Jason's announcement. She knew how much Piper adored Chipper. She'd been so excited to get him.

"Hopefully the little guy will be okay." She motioned toward the kitchen. "It's getting on to dinner time. I've gotten in the habit of cooking lately, but no one else is here to share it with. Can I tempt you with some spaghetti and garlic knots? I've got fresh tea and pop, too."

"Oh, man. That sounds great. But Tashya would kill me. I'm taking her to that fancy new seafood place off Salmon River Road tonight. Rain check maybe?"

"Of course. Wouldn't want your new bride to get mad at you already." She smiled to hide her disappointment. She really missed not having Macon here to share tonight's meal. "Guess I'll make myself a sandwich. No point in going to all that work for one person."

"Sorry, Emma."

"Hey, you're doing me a favor. Saving me a lot of trouble. Why don't you head on home to Tashya now? I'm sure whoever is assigned second shift will be here soon."

"No way. Macon would have my head if I left before he gets here."

"Macon's coming back? Tonight?"

"That's my understanding. Is that a problem? You sound worried."

"No, just surprised. I, ah, said a few things in anger earlier without really thinking it through. I didn't think he'd want to see me again after that."

He blinked, suddenly looking uncomfortable. "I haven't heard anything about that. But I do know he was insistent when he made up the schedule that he be the person here for the night shift. He said if someone tried to bust into your place again he wanted to be here to take them down." He motioned over his shoulder. "Speaking of Macon, I forgot to check the RV. I'll walk the grounds one more time so I can be doubly sure there isn't any sign of another trespasser. I want to be able to answer any questions Macon has when he gets here. You have my cell. Call if you need me. I won't be far."

"Thanks, Jason."

With the news that Macon was coming over, Emma headed into the kitchen and started making the spaghetti she'd originally offered Jason. If Macon had already eaten before he got here, she could easily reheat the spaghetti later. Piper and Barbara would enjoy it for lunch tomorrow. But she hoped he hadn't eaten, because he deserved a hot, home-cooked meal. And an apology.

The sound of a car engine out front half an hour later had both her and Bogie rushing to the front window. Jason's SUV was hurrying down the driveway. No doubt he was eager to take his new love out on the town as promised. Another SUV was parked right out front. And moments later, a very tall, buff, gorgeous male stood in her doorway, practically stealing her breath.

"Macon. Hi, it's good to see you."

He arched a brow in surprise. "I'm here for the next shift. But if it makes you uncomfortable, I can get one of the others to switch with me."

"Not at all. Come in." She opened the door for him, which was sad given that he would normally knock and just come in without waiting. That was her fault, that their easy camaraderie had suffered. Hopefully she could fix it.

When he stepped inside, he locked the door behind him, then set a backpack on the floor at the end of the couch and knelt down to pat Bogie before taking a seat. He glanced up as Emma sat in the chair across from him, his expression stoic, unreadable. "I hope Bogie's still improving. I know I've been sporadic about training with him."

"He's doing great. Piper and I both worked with him today. And I can well understand your hours being unpredictable. I know you've been working really hard."

He frowned, as if confused, or maybe just surprised, by her declaration. But he nodded anyway and glanced around. "Is Angel sleeping?"

She smiled. "Just like the angel that she is. I fed her and put her down just a little while ago. Speaking of which, I just made some spaghetti. I can pop some garlic knots in the oven, too. It'll only take a few minutes. Want me to fix you a plate?" She stood to cross to the kitchen.

"No thanks," he said. "I appreciate it, really. It smells wonderful in here. But I had a quick bite with the chief downtown while we reviewed the case."

She slowly sat back down. "Okay. Well, if you get hungry later, I'll be sure to portion it out in different containers to make it easy to reheat."

"Thanks." He patted Bogie's head again. The shepherd had parked himself at Macon's feet and kept pressing his nose against his jeans.

Emma chuckled. "You'd think he never got any attention the way he acts. But I swear he gets more attention than any of the other animals around here. He's spoiled."

Macon ruffled his fur. "He deserves to be spoiled, don't ya, Bogie?"

Bogie's deep bark filled the room.

"Shh, not in the house." Macon scratched the top of the dog's head. "Not unless there's a bad guy outside."

Emma stood, hating the awkwardness between them. He'd barely looked at her since coming inside. Maybe she'd wait for a better time to apologize. "I'm going to put the spaghetti up. Want a beer? Or tea?"

"I'll get myself something later. Thanks." He grabbed his backpack and unzipped it. "If you don't mind, I'm going to sit here and look over some paperwork."

Just like strangers. All polite and distant.

"Of course. You can use my office if you want."

"No need." He pulled a thick folder out and set it on the couch beside him.

Emma slowly sat back down. "Is that the case file? On Angel?"

He glanced up at her. "One of them. Everything we've got fills a lot more than this folder. Mostly, this has the latest status updates, plus the reports on the break-in."

"I see. I, ah, spoke to Cal about the investigation. He mentioned you have a lot of people you're looking into, like ones associated with me, back when I was fostering pretty regularly. Mind telling me who you're looking at? Maybe I could help. I can tell you about each person, what I remember, anyway."

"I'd planned on talking to you once I narrowed the list down a little more. I suppose I can show you the list now. If someone strikes you as more likely than the others to be involved in something criminal, let me know." He flipped through the thick folder and pulled out a piece of paper.

She took it, her eyes widening. "This is some list. I only fostered a dozen or so kids over the years. There must be—"

"Thirty-seven names. It's the people you fostered plus others we've linked them to with criminal records."

"And there are males and females. I guess this covers potential moms who left Angel, as well as guys who might have tried to break in?"

He nodded. "It could have been a woman who tried breaking in. But given the large shoeprints we saw, it's doubtful. Once the DNA comes back on the blood sample we collected, at least we'll know for sure whether a man or a woman left Angel here. But we still can't assume the two incidents were done by the same person. So we have to keep an open mind, look at every lead, every potential suspect, until we can clear them or move them higher up in priority so we can focus more on them."

"That's a ton of work. Let's see…" She scanned the list, smiling at some of the good memories many of the names evoked. "You can cross these first four off right now. I know all of them even though only that first one was one of my fosters. They're as honest as they come and would never be involved in anything criminal."

"I won't cross them off but I'll note them as a lower priority." He handed her his pen from the side table. "Put an *L* by those and any others you feel strongly about."

She was able to put an *L* by a good third of them, but a few of the names had her grimacing. "This one, Ricky Enos, he was my one for-sure failure. I never could gain his trust. I put up with his bad behavior for a while, but after he stole a few hundred dollars from Barbara's purse, it was out of my hands. He went to juvie. Never heard from him again after that."

"Put an *H* by him," Macon said. "But I remember the name. I'm pretty sure I already have a ton of information on him back at the station."

Her guilt from earlier was riding her hard as she reviewed other names and Macon commented on several of them. Just as Cal had said, Macon and his team had done a lot more investigating than she'd given them credit for. But it still bothered her that William, Hugh and Kyle were still mentioned with the others. They seemed more in need of support than suspicion.

"Here are a few more I'll note as high priority," she said as she marked the page. "I always tried to meet my fosters' friends so I could try to steer my kids away from bad influences." She read off the names she'd just marked. "Maria Loretto. David Timmons. Kelvin Armstrong. Josh Basham. He hung out a lot with Wanda Mickelson. The two of them were a terror, but Josh finally came around and broke up with her. Still, she was a bad influence and he struggled. I don't know what happened to him later. He's probably someone you should look at. Oh, look, Celia Banks is on here. I haven't thought about her in ages. She was so sweet. Like Josh, she had an on-again, off-again relationship with a bad influence. Sean something." She frowned. "Hopper. Yeah, I'll write his name here as someone to look at, high priority. Celia's an *L* for sure, though." She updated the sheet and handed the paper and pen to Macon.

"Thanks." He slid the paper into the folder and flipped back to the front. "I'll look over those later, after I review the status reports."

"I'm sorry."

He frowned. "That I have to review the reports?"

"No. I mean, yes, actually. I'm sorry that you're having to work so hard. You're clearly exhausted. Did you not take a nap today?"

He leaned back against the couch. "Haven't had time. I'll catch up on my sleep tonight."

"You're welcome to use the bed in the second guest room, the one that doubles as my office. It's on the left down the hall."

"I appreciate it. I probably will. Later." He started reading one of the papers in the folder.

"Macon?"

"Hmm?"

"Can you look at me please?"

He glanced at her in question.

"I am so, so sorry for how I acted earlier. For how

I spoke to you. I know better, know how police work is, as I've said before. I never should have second-guessed how you're handling the investigation, or that you *are* handling it. That was wrong of me and, well, I'm really sorry."

He shook his head. "Don't apologize. We're both tired and maybe not as tactful as we'd otherwise be right now. But you said what you felt, can't fault you for that. Did it tick me off? Sure. But I'd rather have honesty than false emotions any day of the week. And I've always gotten honesty from you."

She blinked. "But I was terrible."

He shrugged. "You had valid concerns. Besides, didn't we agree never to apologize?"

"Not if I'm a jerk."

He grinned. "Apology accepted then."

She rolled her eyes, then laughed. "You made that way too easy. I thought you were furious with me."

"Fury is way too strong. I was angry, no doubt. But that was this morning. I'm past that now."

"But when you came in, you didn't even smile. Are you sure you aren't still mad?"

He blew out a deep breath. "I'm not mad. I'm tired. I got about two hours of sleep last night because I was up late, then got your call. It's not personal. Promise."

"Then we're good?"

He smiled, a real smile that lit up his eyes and had her heart swelling in her chest. "We're good."

She stood again, feeling so much better and relieved he'd forgiven her. "Well, okay. I'll go put up dinner now. And I'll bring you back an iced tea. Going through that thick folder is bound to work up your thirst."

Emma was so relieved to have cleared the air between them that she was grinning like a fool the entire time she worked on the kitchen. Bogie chomped on the food she gave him and curled up in the corner a few minutes later on the dog bed she'd brought in.

Once all the food was put up and the kitchen was spotless again, she made the promised iced tea and headed into the family room. And once again she was left holding the glass. Macon was sound asleep, still sitting upright on the couch.

The case folder was in serious danger of falling off his lap onto the floor. Emma managed to rescue it just before it fell, without spilling the tea, which she felt was quite a feat. After setting both the folder and the glass out of harm's way, she stood looking down at him.

The man was too handsome by far. She loved how he kept just enough stubble to form a light beard and mustache that were barely there. Her fingers itched to trace the angles of his face, feel the scratchiness of the stubble beneath them. If she had free rein, she'd smooth her hands up the sides of his head and bury them in the upswept hair on top. Of course, if she was really allowing herself to fantasize, she'd have to admit that she'd like to rip that shirt off over his head and feast her eyes on the muscles underneath. There was a tantalizing glimpse of a tattoo on his left biceps, barely visible beneath the edges of his collared shirt. She'd love to see the whole tattoo and find out whether he had any more.

She shivered and bit her lip. This was crazy. Macon was exhausted and sleeping and here she was ogling him like a Peeping Tom. He deserved his privacy. And she needed to get a grip on her infatuation with him. That's what it was, no denying it. She was completely infatuated with him. And she hadn't even realized how hung up on him she was until she'd spent the entire day feeling horrible for how she'd treated him. She'd felt guilty because she cared about his feelings, and she regretted hurting him. If she didn't care so much, she sure wouldn't have felt so bad all day.

Stop it, Emma. Just stop it.

She had to rein in her fascination with him before it was too late. She'd loved and lost too many people in her life already. And the last man she'd thought she'd loved had gotten her in trouble with the law and nearly destroyed her. He'd broken her trust, broken *her*. It had taken years to get over that. No, she'd do well to remember the lessons of the past. Don't risk your heart and you won't get hurt. Period. She had a life here, a good life, a satisfying life. And she didn't have to have a man in it to make her feel fulfilled.

Macon was a friend, a very good friend. But that's all she could allow him to be.

Which meant, she needed to head back to her office. Or better yet go check on Angel instead of mooning after a man who would never be hers.

Still, he looked so uncomfortable slouched back like that with his head at an awkward angle. She grabbed a pillow from the other end of the couch and carefully tucked it up under his chin. Was it too cold in here? The cold snap earlier had given way to warmer temps again, so she had the air-conditioning on. She pulled the quilted throw from one of the other chairs and gently covered him.

In spite of her vow to keep everything in the friendship zone, she couldn't resist one last thing. She leaned down and ever so softly pressed a kiss against his cheek. A pleasant shiver ran down her spine. Just touching Macon's face was enough to make her dizzy with pleasure. This infatuation was bad, really bad. And she needed to do everything she could to fight it until he did what everyone else she'd ever loved did. Left her. But when Macon left, she promised herself it would be with her heart and her pride intact.

MACON SLOWLY OPENED his eyes, watching Emma leave the room and turn down the hallway. Being woken up with a kiss wasn't something he'd ever have expected, certainly not after the way things had been going today. Part of him wanted to jump up and follow her, kiss her the way he'd always wanted to. But that insanity was quickly squelched by the fact that he was so exhausted he wasn't even sure he could get up. His eyes closed and he drifted back to sleep.

Chapter Thirteen

No one was slowing down with Emma's case, least of all Macon. It had been a long day of interviews and dead ends. He was more than ready to return to Emma's, maybe do some training with Bogie to burn off some of the tension inside him. He was on his way there right now, having gone home only to shower and change clothes.

Even though technically he was off the clock now, he was driving his police-issued SUV in his continued hope of using it as a warning sign to would-be intruders. Would Emma be glad to see him? Hard to say after how they'd left things.

Yes, they'd supposedly made their peace with each other last night. But this morning, their conversations had been stilted and awkward. Emma must have spent most of the night mulling over what had happened, because she kept apologizing. That had him apologizing to her for making her feel like she even needed to apologize. What a mess. He'd tried to assure her that it was okay. And it really was. He understood how she felt. Someone going through the things she'd experienced had every right to be upset. It was just unfortunate that he'd been so tired he let himself get angry in response. Being tired was never an excuse to act in a way that upset someone else. He should have been more understanding.

Hopefully they could move past this blip and go back to the easy friendship they shared. Although more and more, he was having trouble separating that friendship from the idea of something far more intimate and lasting. Especially since Emma had awakened him with that far too chaste kiss. He hadn't mentioned it, not wanting to embarrass her since she obviously hadn't intended for him to even know about it. But he couldn't quit thinking about it and wondering what it meant, and wishing for so much more. Which was really confusing since a few days ago she'd talked about them going back to the ways things used to be, meaning just friends, once the case was resolved. Was she fighting their attraction for a reason he didn't know about? Or did she truly not want to be more than friends?

He shook his head, not sure what to make of everything. It didn't seem possible that so little time had passed since they'd come back into each others' lives. And that so much had changed inside him as a result. Where before, he'd been hurting and wanted nothing more than to be by himself, now he couldn't imagine a day without Emma in it. But until he resolved the investigations around Angel and the attempted break-in, there wasn't any point in thinking about pursuing a relationship. Above everything else, he needed to focus on what was most important— keeping Emma safe and getting Angel back to her family.

He knew from experience that all it would take was one solid lead to break the investigation wide open. But the problem was they had so many tips, generated from the flyers around town and knock-and-talks he and his team had conducted throughout Jasper, that it was nearly impossible to weed out any real tips from the noise.

He turned onto Emma's driveway and hit the brakes. What was going on? Was the entire police force here? There were SUVs and police-issued sedans end to end in the circular drive in front of her house. And several more squeezed in between some trees by Piper's and Barbara's vehicles. If someone had hurt Emma and no one had called him, there'd be hell to pay.

He zipped up the driveway, coming to a rocking halt behind the last vehicle. He was almost to the front porch when the door opened and Barbara stepped out, cradling Angel in her arms. Weaving around her feet was a little corgi puppy.

"Hey, Macon. I saw your SUV through the window."

"Hi, Barbara. Who's that little guy trying to eat your shoes?"

"Eat my...oh good grief. Stop it, Chipper." She

chuckled and pushed him back inside before pulling the door closed behind her. "That's Piper's new puppy. He swallowed something he shouldn't have and ended up at the vet's. He's doing okay but she wanted him close by so she can check on him when she takes breaks. Are you looking for Emma? If so, she's in the training ring out back."

He frowned. "The training ring? Then, nothing happened? Nothing's wrong?"

"What do you—oh, all the police cars." She grinned. "Amazing isn't it, how loved and accepted Emma is in the police community? Apparently after everyone recovered from yesterday's antics they wanted to come over and show their support for Emma and DCA. It's practically a county fair out there. Go on. Everything's fine. If Angel and I need anything, which I'm sure we won't, we'll holler out the back door."

He hesitated, thinking about the various leads he and his fellow officers were wading through. With all the police cars out front, the likelihood of anyone trying to break into the house right now was about zero. But still. He didn't want Barbara left unprotected if someone was intent on coming after Angel.

"Where's Bogie? Is he out back, too?"

"No, he's inside with Jason. We're totally secure here. You're welcome to come in if you want."

Relief eased the tension in his shoulders. "No, that's good. Just wanted to make sure all was well. Thanks."

He strode around the left side of the house. County

fair seemed an apt description as he stopped to take everything in. Emma was sitting on her Appaloosa in the middle of the ring. Piper was several yards away, walking down a row of happy-looking K-9s. Most of them were perfectly behaved, sitting and staying as instructed. Two, a pair of black Labs he remembered were being trained for a SAR team in Boise, were anything but obeying orders. Instead of sitting, they were doing their own version of search-and-rescue, pouncing on anything that moved in the dirt. Macon chuckled as they both went for a drag-onfly and fell on top of each other.

Their audience, sitting on top of or lounging against the white three-rail fence, egged the Labs on, laughing and whistling.

Piper aimed an exasperated look at the worst of-fenders in her audience, who simply shrugged and laughed. She rolled her eyes and went after the two rebel K-9s, determined to get them to line up with the others.

Macon waited by the back deck, taking inventory of everyone there, human and otherwise. He was surprised to see Chief Walters with his K-9, Buddy. The dog's face was so white and he was so slow get-ting up and down these days that he was basically already retired. He was also mostly deaf and none of the shenanigans were making a dent in his nap as he lay on the grass at the chief's feet.

Even more surprising than seeing the chief here was that the office manager, Theresa Norwood, was there. She rarely ever left the office. It was her own little fiefdom. But then again, she was the chief's shadow. If he was out having fun, she was usually with him. There was no secret that she was head over heels for him and he for her. But they'd never admit it and seemed to think no one else knew.

Cal Hoover was there with his German shepherd, Ruby, whom Emma had trained years ago. Brady Nichols had his yellow lab, Winnie, sitting at his feet. And while their best detective, Margaret Avery, didn't have a K-9, the rookie beside her, Ava Callan, did. Her dog was yet another German shepherd, Lacey.

A few of the officers and K-9s weren't there, like Jenny in dispatch. No doubt she was at the station, handling the phones until the night shift dispatcher arrived. Dillon Diaz wasn't there either, but he probably would have been if he could be. Like most at Jasper PD, he was a fan of the Daniels Canine Academy. Emma had not only trained most of the dogs for their police department, she'd worked with charities and did fundraisers to purchase and pay for the training. Since police-quality trained K-9s could run anywhere from a few thousand dollars to nearly twenty, depending on how specialized they were, that was no small savings. The little town of Jasper had a higher K-9 to human officer ratio than any other department in Idaho because of Emma's firm belief in the benefits of having K-9s in law enforcement.

The one person not here who was definitely no

surprise was Captain Rutledge. He alone was the voice *against* the K-9 program. He disliked dogs in general and felt they were a distraction from what he called "real" police work. His attitude was puzzling, given that the Jasper K-9s had saved so many lives over the years. And they were critical to the success of the drug enforcement efforts in the county. But Rutledge made no secret that he'd eliminate the program once he became chief.

If he became chief.

Rutledge seemed to think it was a foregone conclusion that once Walters retired, he would take his place. And it did seem as if the chief was leaning that way. Again, understandable since Rutledge was so smart and had an incredible knack for strategic planning. His photographic memory and ability to solve problems was a gift. And he knew it. But his condescending attitude and lack of interpersonal skills meant that most of the officers couldn't stand to be around him.

Macon had tried not to let the whispers and gripes around the station influence his own opinion of Rutledge. But the man seemed to go out of his way to try to annoy Macon. Maybe it was his way of razzing the new guy. But that high school bully attitude had no place in a professional environment where trusting your fellow officer could mean the difference between life and death. Macon, like many others, fervently hoped that the chief chose someone else to succeed him.

Macon headed toward the others. A cheer went up just as he leaned against the fence. At first he thought his fellow officers were teasing him for finally showing up. But they weren't cheering *him*. They were cheering Emma. She was taking her bows at the end of the K-9 line beside the two rebellious Labs. Both of them were now sitting upright like the other dogs, the picture of perfect obedience.

Piper was shaking her head, but grinning. She bowed in deference to Emma's training expertise, then mounted the Appaloosa.

Macon leaned against the fence beside Cal. "Why is the horse there?"

Cal nodded in greeting. "I'm not really sure. I thought Emma had taken the horse out for exercise. But then Piper brought out the dogs. It's impressive, isn't it? How the horse doesn't shy away from the dogs even when they bark? And the dogs don't mind the horse even when Emma had it trotting around the ring earlier."

"Desensitizing training."

Cal gave him a funny look. "What?"

"Special training Emma does to keep the animals comfortable in certain situations, like around sudden loud noises. Since she trains K-9s for a variety of police departments, they need to be conditioned to work around horses in case they ever work with equestrian units."

"Makes sense, I suppose."

"In addition to training all the dogs on the basics of

police work and taking down bad guys, she specializes in scent training for some of the dogs, for drug detection and bomb-sniffing. It just depends on the needs of the department that owns each dog. That yellow Lab on the end is going to work with a bomb unit in McCall. She and Piper just finished certifying a bloodhound for search-and-rescue. They take turns hiding in the foothills past the kennels and teach dogs to find them and alert on their position." He was going to say more, but when he glanced at Cal again, he saw him grinning and shaking his head. "What's so amusing?"

Cal chuckled. "It's just that you've been with Jasper PD for all of a hot minute. I've been here for years. Emma trained my dog, all of our dogs except the chief's old guy, Buddy. And you're telling me what types of training she does. It's just…funny. It's also telling."

Macon turned to face him. "Telling?"

"You like her."

Macon snorted and turned back toward the fence. "All of Jasper PD likes her or they wouldn't be here showing their support."

"Um-hmm."

"Shut up, Cal."

Cal laughed and clasped him on the shoulder. "See you tomorrow, Macon. The wife and kids are waiting dinner on me. I'd say take good care of Emma when we all leave, but I know you will. Come on, Ruby. Heel."

He was laughing as he headed toward his car with his K-9 trotting happily alongside him.

Macon greeted a few of the others but his attention was mainly centered on the incredibly gifted woman putting the dogs through their paces for her audience. He didn't know who had organized this impromptu session, but the happiness on Emma's face was the reward. He didn't realize how stressed the recent events had made her until he saw her like this, with her guard down, just enjoying life. Which had him itching to get back to his case files. He wanted this thing done, closed, so she could continue to laugh and smile the way she was right now.

Then she looked at him.

Her smile, if anything, became more bright. Her eyes danced with pleasure as she gave him a wave. Someone next to him shoved him good-naturedly and he returned Emma's wave. They could tease him all they wanted. All he cared about right now was seeing more of that smile of hers. And making her safe.

"Why didn't anyone tell me we were having a party?"

Macon stiffened at the unwelcome voice behind him. The ring went silent. The smiles on everyone's faces disappeared.

Captain Rutledge had shown up after all.

Chapter Fourteen

When Rutledge arrived at the training ring, Emma could have sworn the temperature outside dropped ten degrees. She hadn't spoken to him much over the years and he hadn't sought her out, no doubt because of his reputation of complaining that the K-9 program was too much overhead for a small police force like Jasper's. Never mind that the initial cost of obtaining each dog had been covered by Emma's fundraising efforts. Or that her continued fundraising provided reduced-cost veterinarian care to the K-9s. And that the officers themselves footed the bills for their food. None of that seemed to sway Rutledge's negative opinion. Still, even knowing his views, and having heard officers complain about him, it had been shocking to see the negative effect he had on their morale the moment he'd appeared.

Rutledge was speaking to Chief Walters and Cal Hoover about something. The other officers had edged away from the group. Emma glanced at Macon, curious about his reaction. His expression appeared to be carefully blank, but he, too, had moved away from the trio. Was it to give them privacy? Or because he didn't want to be near Rutledge, either? He pulled out his cell phone and looked at the screen before putting the phone to his ear. Maybe he'd stepped away to take a call.

Everyone's reactions to the captain had her wondering about the rumors that Walters was going to choose Rutledge as his successor. From what she'd seen, Hoover inspired much more respect from his fellow officers. And he got along with everyone. Of course, Emma was biased. Cal had been a friend of her father's. And he was a huge supporter of her K-9 program.

Whatever Rutledge had come here to discuss must have been important, because all three men—Rutledge, the chief and Cal—turned and headed toward their cars. The station manager, Theresa, nudged Buddy awake and snapped a leash onto his collar. She gently urged the aging dog along, then stopped to tell Macon something. He nodded and she headed to her car, too.

"Emma, are we going to do more training today?" Piper asked as she crossed the ring. She'd just finished putting Elton back in his stall.

Emma glanced at the remaining officers, gauging their interest. But Rutledge's appearance, and the chief and Cal leaving, had changed the atmosphere. It was getting late anyway. She'd thoroughly enjoyed the camaraderie and levity her unexpected visitors had created. It was a welcome respite from the stress she'd been under. But that was over now. However, it didn't have to be over forever. She had an idea of how she could recapture that closeness and fun again.

"We're done for today," she told Piper. "If you'll lead the dogs back inside, I'll be there in a few minutes to help feed them and settle them down for the night."

"Sounds good." Piper opened the gate at the far end of the ring that led directly into the kennel building. A quick command and the dogs came running. The ones more toward the end of their training at DCA were more sedate and calm about leaving the ring. The rest of them, particularly the two SAR Labs, lost all signs of decorum and were barking and spinning around like a circus act.

Piper resorted to bribing the last of the stragglers with treats to get them to leave the ring. A few smiles and scattered laughs followed her departure. But it was clear everyone was getting ready to leave.

Emma hurried to the fence to catch them before they took off. "Thank you all for coming. It was an unexpected pleasure. You're welcome to stop by any time. And if you ever want refresher training for you and your K-9 partners, please let me know and I'll get you on the schedule. I'd also like to make an announcement. Since the DCA ten-year anniversary celebration we had several months ago was so fun, I've decided to make it an annual affair. I hope you'll all come for the eleventh anniversary party next year."

A cheer went up and she laughed. "We'll make

it even bigger and better than the last one. I'd like to plan a K-9 skill demonstration for you and your families, too. Is that something you'd like?"

Macon smiled and nodded as the others assured her they'd love it.

"Great. Since I've never put on an official demonstration before, I'll have to plan everything out and get some practice in ahead of time. Would anyone be interested in an anniversary-planning cookout in a month or two? I might even make some of my mom's famous huckleberry pie."

The enthusiastic response to her impromptu plan was so overwhelming that she was wiping away tears of gratitude in between the hugs and offers of help. She was still trying to hide her tears and wipe her eyes as the last of the officers drove away; everyone, that is, except Macon. He took one look at her tear-streaked face and immediately climbed over the three-rail fence and dropped down at her side. Before she could ask him what he was doing, he gently pulled her against his chest and wrapped his arms around her.

The hug was so unexpected, but so wonderful, that she immediately sank into the embrace and tightened her arms around his waist.

"It's okay, Emma," he whispered against the top of her head as he gently rubbed her back. "I know you're under tremendous stress right now. But I promise this is all going to end soon. I'm doing everything I can to find Angel's family and catch whoever tried to break into your home. And until I do, I'll make sure you're never alone. Okay?"

She blinked in surprise, still hugging him close. "Thank you, Macon."

"Any time."

Rather than correct his assumption that she'd cried because of stress or fear, she decided to let him think that was the cause. Mainly because she didn't want to end the hug to tell him.

The tears were because she was so overwhelmed by the acceptance and love she'd received today. She'd always felt close and friendly with the Jasper PD officers. But the way they'd circled the wagons to help her in her time of need was beyond anything she'd have ever expected. It had her missing Rick and Susan so much. But it also had her so very grateful for the people in her life, and newly aware that there were more people who cared about her than she'd ever realized.

And one of them, whether he admitted it openly or not, was Macon.

That shouldn't matter. In spite of all her admonitions to herself that she didn't want to risk her heart, or risk getting hurt, she didn't want this hug to end. But she'd held on to him so long it was going to get awkward if she didn't let go soon. And Piper would start wondering why she hadn't gone to the kennels yet to help her.

She loosened her arms and pulled back to thank him for caring, for wanting to make sure she was okay. But the second she looked up into those warm brown eyes staring down at her with raw male hunger, she was lost. She didn't know which of them reached for the other first, but suddenly they were in each other's arms and she was happily drowning in the hottest, most all-consuming kiss she'd ever experienced.

Holy fry sauce, did this man know how to stoke a fire.

He was so gentle, achingly sweet. And yet there was a raw hunger she sensed in him, just beneath the surface, as if he was struggling to hold himself back. This wasn't a man who wanted to overpower her with his strength and size. Instead, he was focused on giving her pleasure and allowing her to take it as far as she was willing to go. That combination, his focus on her needs, was heady, like a drug. And she wanted more, so much more.

She slid her greedy fingers across his face, reveling in the raspiness of the light stubble as her tongue dueled with his. He groaned low in his throat and tightened his hold, answering her hunger with more of his own. The beauty of it nearly made her weep. She could not get enough of this incredible man.

"Hey, Emma, are you—oh! Sorry! My bad."

Piper's voice was like a bucket of ice water across Emma's nerve endings. She jerked back from Macon and whirled around just in time to see Piper ducking into the kennel building. She groaned.

Macon laughed.

She turned back to face him and couldn't help laughing too. "That was…"

"Amazing?"

"Unexpected."

"I like amazing better," he said.

"How about hot?"

He grinned. "Definitely hot."

He was about to say something else when his phone buzzed in his pocket. His eyes widened in dismay. "Ah, shoot. I forgot." He yanked the phone out and checked the screen. "I'm so sorry, Emma. I need to take this. It's important." He stepped a few feet away. "Hello, yeah. No, I haven't left yet. Okay, yes."

Emma sighed and lifted a shaky hand to adjust her ponytail, which had come half-undone. Her heart was still racing and she drew slow, deep breaths trying to regain control. As Macon continued to talk to whoever was on the other end of the phone, she looked over her shoulder. No sign of Piper, but Emma knew what she was doing. Feeding and watering a dozen dogs, making sure their enclosures were clean and locking things up for the night. And she shouldn't have to do all of that alone. Guilt had her wanting to race to the building. But she couldn't run off without wrapping up whatever had just happened. And how exactly did one wrap up after that earth-tilting kiss? Should she just say, *hey, thanks, see ya later*?

She chuckled and he looked at her, a brow arched in question. But since he was still talking on the phone, she simply stood and waited for him to finish.

Finally, he shoved the phone back in his pocket and crossed to her. "I really hate to—"

"Rock my world, then take off?"

He grinned with obvious male satisfaction. "Something like that." His smile faded. "A little earlier I got a lead in the investigation. I arranged for Jason to stay a little while longer and was supposed to meet my contact a few minutes ago. But I got distracted by all the activity in the ring. You put on an amazing show, by the way."

"Thanks. It was spur-of-the-moment but a ton of fun."

"It was. I really have to go, Emma. But I'll be back in a couple of hours. We should probably talk about what just happened. I know it was completely inappropriate since I'm supposed to be protecting you, not taking advantage of—"

"Don't," she told him. "Don't you dare say it was a mistake. Do what you need to do. But don't ruin a kiss like that with an apology."

"Emma—"

She waggled her fingers in the air in answer as she hurried toward the kennels.

Chapter Fifteen

Macon passed a slow-moving car, anxious to return to Emma's place. He'd been gone much longer than he'd meant to, but at least he knew Jason was there watching after her. Having Jason's police car parked in front of the house was a great deterrent, but Macon wouldn't feel completely secure about her safety unless he was there.

His hands tightened on the steering wheel. At least he'd made some progress tonight. He could finally cross Hugh and William off his list of people connected to Angel *and* the break-in attempt. His source's information had been spot-on about where the teens would be tonight. That had allowed Macon to surprise them and he'd finally gotten to confront them about inconsistencies in their stories. A few calls later and he'd corroborated their alibis. They were in the clear.

Kyle Norvell, on the other hand, definitely was *not* in the clear.

The kid was avoiding him at every turn. He hadn't shown up for his most recently scheduled work days at DCA. And his parents were covering for him, making excuses. If they'd just get Kyle to sit down with him and be honest about where he kept disappearing every night, per the tip that Macon had received from William, then Kyle could be cleared, too.

Or he could become the number one suspect.

He glanced at the clock on the SUV's dash and grimaced. He needed to reassure Jason that he'd be there soon. The kid was a newlywed and would be champing at the bit to get home. This wasn't the first time he'd been late because of Macon. He'd have to make it up to Jason by assigning someone else his shift tomorrow.

Pulling to the shoulder of the road to make the call, he got out his phone, then frowned. He'd turned it off earlier tonight, not wanting to risk any noise that might alert the teens as he sneaked up on their little campsite in the woods. He'd meant to turn it back on when he'd left and had forgot.

As soon as he powered it up, messages started filling his screen. He chuckled when he saw all of them were from Jason, and most of them were telling him that Tashya was going to put him in the doghouse if he didn't get home soon.

When Macon read Jason's last message, he swore. Tashya's parents were at her and Jason's house for a visit and she'd insisted he come home. The young rookie had made the assumption, based on Macon's original plan on when he'd return, that it would be okay to head home. He'd reasoned that Macon would arrive a few minutes after he left, so he hoped it would be all right.

Hell, no, it was *not* all right.

Jason had left two hours ago. Other than Bogie, there was no one else there protecting Emma.

He swore again and was just about to call Emma when she called him. Relief flooded through him as he answered and pulled back onto the road.

"Emma, hey. Sorry for the delay. I'm on my way and—"

"Macon. Someone's on the property. They must have broken into the kennel buildings. The dogs are loose and running all over the place. Should I call 911?"

A cold chill ran down Macon's spine. He slammed the accelerator, making the SUV jump forward. "Have you seen anyone? Have they tried to break inside?"

"No. All I've seen, and heard, are the dogs. I suppose Piper could have accidentally left the main gate open. But each of the kennels inside also has a gate. It's hard to imagine her being that careless."

"Agreed. Someone's definitely behind this. They're probably trying to draw you outside. Where are you?"

"The family room right now. I put Angel in her crib and grabbed my pistol. I turned out all the lights and have been peeking through the blinds. Jason already left. Bogie's inside, with me."

He was totally going to murder Jason Wright.

"Good. Stay inside. Call 911, but I'm not waiting

around. I'm almost there. Might as well take advantage of this opportunity to try to sneak up and catch whoever is terrorizing you. Let Jenny know I'll park my SUV on Elm Street, just before the entrance to DCA. She'll need to alert the other officers to go in silent and be aware there's an armed officer already on the premises. I'd rather not get hit by friendly fire."

"Macon, maybe you should wait. I don't want you to get hurt."

The concern in her voice was almost his undoing. He wanted nothing more than to run inside the house and hold her close, to see for himself that she was safe. But being in fear every day was no way to live. He needed to end this. So instead, he tried to reassure her, even as he crept along the tree line on the left side of the property.

"That's my job, Emma. Don't worry about me. I'm going in on foot so I don't scare the intruder off. Stay inside, keep the doors locked. If anything, and I mean *anything* happens that makes you worry about your own safety, call me and barricade yourself with Angel in her room. I'll come running."

"Thanks, Macon. And please, please be careful."

"You too. Make that call. I'm at DCA now."

"Calling dispatch."

He left the phone and ringer on this time, just in case Emma needed to call him. It's not like it would add much to the noise outside if it did ring. The dogs were barking and he could see several of them off in the distance, milling around the outside of the kennel building and the barn. Hopefully they wouldn't come running toward him and give away his presence until he figured out where the intruder was— assuming they were still on the property. He was betting they were and that the stunt with the dogs was to trick Emma into going outside—especially since there wasn't a police car parked in front of her house anymore.

Jason would be lucky to have a job tomorrow once Macon was through with him.

Banking on the assumption that the dogs were hanging around the outbuildings because that's where the intruder was, he hurried toward that location, using the trees, bushes and darkness for cover.

His weapon was drawn and he had a small flashlight at the ready to flick on and illuminate a target.

A distant bark sounded from inside the house. Bogie. He was getting nervous. Either he'd sensed the intruder, or he'd sensed Macon. Or maybe backup was already here, following in Macon's footsteps. He needed to find the intruder, fast, before the dogs alerted on anyone else and revealed their positions.

Crouching down behind some trees about ten yards off to the side of the kennels, Macon scanned the outside of the building. There, on the far side nearest the barn, a shadow moved. Was it one of the dogs? No, a dog wouldn't crouch down like that and stay in one spot.

Macon eased around another tree. Closer. Closer. Ten yards away. Nine. Eight.

Suddenly two of the dogs came running toward him, howling like a couple of coyotes. It was the black Labs Piper had struggled to keep under control in the training ring. The shadow by the building jumped up and took off toward the barn.

Macon leaped over the two dogs and sprinted after him. "Police, stop!" He snapped the flashlight on as he rounded the barn.

The fleeing figure was dressed completely in black, with a hoodie covering his head. But he hadn't thought to wear black shoes. The flash of his white sneakers was like a beacon, shining in the beam of Macon's flashlight.

"Stop or I'll shoot," Macon yelled, putting on a burst of speed.

The man ignored him and ran past the barn. He tried to leap over the three-rail fence enclosing the training ring. Instead, he slammed against it and fell in the dirt. He swore and scrambled to his feet, then started climbing.

Macon shoved his pistol in his holster and vaulted over the fence, landing on top of the suspect on the other side. The other man cried out as they both crashed to the ground. The flashlight skittered across the dirt a few feet away.

"Freeze, you scumbag," Macon yelled as he wrestled with the flailing man.

They rolled several times until Macon slammed him onto his stomach. Macon straddled his back and shoved the suspect's right arm up between his shoulder blades.

The suspect cried out in pain. "Okay, okay, please, stop!"

Macon leaned across him and snagged his flashlight. After snatching off the man's hoodie, Macon grabbed his hair and yanked back his head, shining the light on his face.

"Don't shoot! Don't shoot! Please!" Tears streaked down his pale face as he begged for his life.

Macon swore in disgust.

It was Kyle Norvell.

Chapter Sixteen

Emma paced back and forth in her family room, watching the blue and red lights flashing against the closed blinds. Once again her driveway had several Jasper police vehicles. But other than Cal letting her know a few minutes ago that everything was secure and that they were rounding up the K-9s, no one was telling her anything. She was told to wait inside.

It was frustrating not knowing what was happening on her own property. Bogie was handling the situation far better than her. He'd parked himself near the front door, ears cocked forward like a neon sign on top of a taxi saying *on-duty*. No one was getting inside the house unless Bogie let them. Even Cal had been forced to wait to talk to her until she'd ordered Bogie to stand down.

She appreciated the K-9's protection and loyalty. But she didn't appreciate having to wait for more updates. Cal had said Macon caught the suspect and was okay. That was a relief, all the way around. But what did it really mean? He'd caught the suspect who'd let the dogs out? Or the suspect who was responsible for all the strange happenings lately? Most importantly, what did this mean for Angel? Emma had just gotten used to the idea that the person who left her must have been her mother. But would her mother do all these crazy things, like let the dogs out of their kennels?

If this latest occurrence was related to Angel, that could mean the police knew who she belonged to. That could also mean Angel wouldn't be here much longer with Emma taking care of her.

Just thinking about that possibility had her throat tightening and her heart squeezing in her chest. She'd been trying so hard not to become attached. But when you fed, bathed, clothed and cuddled a precious, sweet little baby how the heck were you not supposed to care about her and what might happen to her? She deserved to be loved and cherished, as all children did. Emma didn't know how she was going to survive giving her up. Especially if the parents turned out not to be the caring, loving people the baby deserved.

Calm down. You're making huge leaps in logic. Tonight's events may have nothing to do with Angel.

The motion-sensor floodlights flickered on outside. Voices sounded, along with the crunch of the gravel driveway beneath shoes. She rushed to the front windows. Bogie growled his displeasure as she peeked through the blinds.

"It's okay, boy," she reassured him. "I'm safe. Just trying to see what's happening."

As she watched, four Jasper police officers rounded the end of the house and headed toward one of the police cars. Relief swept through her as she recognized Macon with them. Even though Cal had said Macon was okay, she'd needed to see for herself. Cal was walking beside him. Brady and Dillon took up the rear. And in the middle, with his handcuffed arm being grasped by Macon, was Kyle Norvell.

Emma sucked in a sharp breath. No! Kyle couldn't be the one behind everything. He couldn't be. But as she watched, Macon opened the rear door of the closest police car and forced Kyle inside. Was Macon arresting him?

"Oh no, you don't." She threw open the front door, ignoring Bogie's barks, and jogged down the front steps. "Macon, stop. Let him go."

Macon shut the car door and turned around, frowning down at her. "Emma, you shouldn't be out here. What if Kyle's working with a partner? You could still be in danger." He motioned to Brady. "Get her inside."

Brady hurried to Emma.

A low-throated growl had him stopping as he reached for her. Bogie's teeth were bared as he stood in front of Emma, his hackles raised.

Macon issued a command in German along with "Bogart" and Bogie immediately stopped growling. But he didn't move away from Emma.

Macon exchanged a surprised look with her.

She crossed her arms and arched a brow. "Bogie knows I don't want to go back inside the house and no one is going to force me. Now what's going on? Why is Kyle in handcuffs?"

Macon's eyes narrowed. "Your resident juvenile delinquent is the one who trespassed on your property and let all the dogs out. Tomorrow, after the sun comes up, we'll search for more evidence. I won't be surprised if we find proof that he's the one who tried to break into your house."

A pounding noise sounded behind him.

Kyle was banging on the police car's window, his terrified gaze pleading with Emma.

Macon motioned to Dillon. "Take him to the station. I'll meet you there."

Dillon carefully avoided Bogie and got into the driver's seat.

Emma spoke a low command to Bogie. He ran and vaulted onto the hood of the car, barking and growling as if he was going to dive through the windshield to get Dillon.

"What the—" Macon whirled around toward Emma. "You've broken my dog."

She crossed her arms. "He's not broken. He's loyal to me *and* to you. But if either of us seems to be in danger, he's going to go with his instincts and protect us."

He shook his head in disgust and strode to the car. He gave Bogie a command in German and the dog immediately stopped growling and hopped off the car. Dillon started the engine, but hesitated, watching as Emma started forward.

Macon moved to block her path.

"Don't," she snapped.

"Don't what?"

"Don't let Dillon take Kyle to the station. Let me talk to him." She motioned toward the back window where Kyle was yelling and pleading for help. "He wants to tell us something."

"He wants to save his sorry butt by telling more lies."

"Where's your compassion for a young, scared kid?"

"Compassion? Look at how he's dressed, Emma. All in black so no one would see him in the dark. He had a hoodie pulled over his face to hide his identity. Today's been warm for this time of year so it sure as certain wasn't because he was cold. I found him skulking around the kennel building, hiding in the shadows. When I identified myself as a police officer, he took off running, away from me. What do you think all that means? That he's innocent and just happened to be on a stroll on your property miles from his house at the same time that someone released all your very expensive K-9s?"

Emma's face flushed hot at the lecture. She glanced at Cal and Brady, who'd taken several steps back as if to distance themselves from the discussion.

She cleared her throat. "What if I refuse to press charges?"

Macon's jaw tightened. He motioned to Dillon to cut the engine.

"And why would you do that, Emma?" His voice was hard, cold.

She drew a deep, bracing breath and prayed that she could make him understand. "When I look at Kyle, I see myself. When my foster father was killed in the line of duty, I couldn't cope. I rebelled and fell in with the wrong crowd. I did some stupid, awful things. I deserved to go to jail, maybe even prison. But Chief Walters had compassion for me. He understood what I was going through and gave me a second chance. It's because of that compassion that I turned my life around. Kyle's been through some rocky times, too, and he deserves a second chance. If you arrest him now, the judge could revoke the conditions of his release for his last offense. He could go to prison."

Empathy had flickered in his gaze as she spoke. But when she finished, she could tell by his hard, unyielding look that the empathy wasn't for Kyle. It was for her.

"Kyle isn't you, Emma. And he already had a second chance, working community service at DCA. He threw that away when he trespassed on your property, jeopardizing thousands of dollars' worth of animals. And if he's behind everything else, he's done a heck of a lot more than that. If he ends up in prison, it's because he earned it."

Ignoring their audience, Emma stepped close and

feathered her hand against his cheek. "Like you said, Kyle and I are different. Some people need more than a second chance to turn the corner, to make better choices. Please. Do this for me. Give Kyle an opportunity to explain what he was doing on my property tonight. That's all I'm asking. Just listen to him, *really* listen."

He stared down at her a long moment, his expression unreadable. Then he swore and, with a surprisingly gentle motion, pulled her hand down from his face. "If I do this, and he can't come up with anything plausible to explain his actions, will you agree to press charges?"

She glanced at Kyle's tear-streaked face, remembering another night much like this one when she'd been the one in the back of the police car.

"Emma?"

"I don't know, okay? I just need to hear his side before you lock him away. Please."

Obviously not happy with her reply, he glanced past her at Cal, as if silently asking the more senior officer's opinion. Emma turned to look at Cal, too, but Macon was already heading to the driver's door of the police car. He tapped on the window.

Dillon rolled it down, looking at him in question.

"Change of plans," Macon said. "We're going to interview Kyle here first. *Then* we'll take him to the station."

Macon issued a command to Bogie. Then he stalked to Emma and gestured toward the house.

"I'm not convinced that Kyle doesn't have a partner in crime lurking in the trees out here watching what's going on. Let's take this inside where you'll be safe."

She glanced past the reach of the floodlights to the darkened silhouettes of trees at the edge of her property and suddenly felt very exposed and vulnerable.

Macon grabbed her hand and pulled her toward the steps while Bogie trotted after them.

A few minutes later everyone was seated in the family room and the interrogation had begun. In spite of Emma's protests, Kyle was still in handcuffs. But at least he was on the couch now instead of locked in the back of a patrol car.

Macon held up his hand, stopping Kyle mid-sentence. "That's a load of crap you're selling. You expect me to believe you took your mom's car, left it parked down the street so no one would see it, dressed like a burglar and sneaked onto this property...*to visit the dogs*?"

"It's the truth! I swear!" Kyle looked at Emma sitting by the fireplace on the other side of the room, his eyes silently pleading for help. Macon had insisted that she stay far away from Kyle, with Bogie once again on guard in front of her in full protection mode. But she wasn't going to ignore what was happening and remain silent.

She smiled reassuringly. "Go on, Kyle, tell Macon everything. He's a reasonable man, but you have to be honest."

Macon gave her an aggravated look, then turned back toward Kyle.

Kyle licked his lips. He nodded at Emma, then straightened instead of cowering against the back of the couch. His cheeks flushed a bright red as he spoke.

"I like the dogs, okay? The horses, too, but I really like the dogs. They don't yell at me or judge me. They're always in a good mood and happy to see me. They make me feel good, you know?" A single tear slid down his cheek and he brushed his face against his shoulder to wipe it away, his face flushing even redder.

"What's that got to do with you sneaking onto the property at night?" Macon demanded. But his voice had lost some of its edge.

"It's stupid, okay? I know it's stupid. But, well, you've been accusing me of things and keep wanting to question me so I've been avoiding you."

"No kidding."

"I've been avoiding you," Kyle continued. "And since you've been here every day, I haven't been able to see the dogs. So I…" He swallowed, looking miserable. "I've been sneaking out here at night to pet them and check on them."

"I don't believe you."

"It's true! I've been visiting them for weeks." His eyes widened at his admission and he aimed an apologetic look at Emma. "I'm sorry, Ms. Daniels. But it's true. I've been sneaking onto your property ever since I started working here. I'm the tough guy, you know? With Hugh and William. I can't act all soft and stuff in front of them. I've never had a dog of my own and they're really cool. I really do love those dogs."

Emma's throat was tight. The pain and embarrassment in his voice had her wanting to cross the room to wrap him in a tight hug. But she didn't dare try, positive that Macon or the others would stop her.

"I know you do, Kyle," she assured him. "You're saying you wanted to see the dogs but didn't want anyone else to know you liked them? Because you thought it would make you seem too soft, too vulnerable, if your friends knew?"

He nodded, looking miserable.

"If that's true, then why let the dogs out of the kennels?" Macon asked. "You endangered them. They could have run off, gone out to the road, maybe been hit by a car."

Kyle's eyes widened. "I didn't let them out. They were already out when I got here. I was going to try to round them up, get them back in their kennels. Then you came running at me so I took off."

"I announced that I was a police officer. Why didn't you stop?"

Kyle rolled his eyes. "You're kidding, right? I knew what would happen if you caught me. You'd assume I'd done something wrong and would throw me in the back of a police car." Kyle aimed a mutinous expression at Macon.

Dillon coughed as if to cover a laugh.

Before Macon could ask another question, Kyle volunteered, "Besides, I couldn't be sure you were a real cop in the dark. It could have been the other guy, trying to trick me."

The room went silent and every eye was suddenly watching Kyle intently.

"What other guy?" Macon asked.

Kyle rolled his eyes again. "Are you even *trying* to listen to me? I told you the dogs were out when I got here. There was another guy skulking around. He ran into the same trees where you came running out. I wasn't sure what to think and took off. But I swear I didn't let any of the dogs out. I was there to check on them. That's it."

Cal stepped forward. "You saw someone else out there tonight, aside from Lieutenant Ridley?"

"Yes, sir. He was wearing dark clothes. Like me. And like I said, he ran into the trees, just past the kennels."

"Kyle," Macon said, recapturing his attention. "Where was this other man when you first saw him?"

"Outside, out back. Running."

"Out back, meaning behind this house?"

"Yeah. He was running across the yard, sprinting past the paddock, the training ring. I ducked behind the kennels and he ran right past me."

"Did you get a good look at him? Did you recognize him?"

He shrugged. "It was pretty dark. I was just trying not to let anyone see me. And I wanted to get the dogs back in their kennels after he was gone, so I was waiting to make sure he'd left."

Cal drew his weapon and tapped Dillon on the shoulder. "Let's check it out." They headed outside.

Macon and Brady exchanged an uneasy glance before Macon continued the questioning. "Kyle, those two officers who just left are going to look for signs of this guy you supposedly saw. Are you wasting their time?"

He vigorously shook his head. "No, I swear. Like I said, I didn't do anything. Except…" His face reddened again and he glanced at Emma before looking down at the floor.

"Except what?" Macon asked.

"It's okay," Emma called out. "Whatever it is, it's okay. Just tell the truth, Kyle."

He let out a shaky breath. "I'm really sorry, Ms. Daniels. I know it was wrong. But I didn't think it would cause any real harm." Another tear slid down his cheek.

"Kyle—" Macon warned.

"I fed the dogs," Kyle blurted out, as if he was admitting to an egregious sin. "I know it's wrong because they belong to other people and all. And some of them are on specific diets. But they're so fun when you give them treats. They jump all over you and lick you and they really enjoy them. I feed them treats every time I sneak onto the property."

"Oh for Pete's sake," Macon said. "This is ridiculous. You do *not* sneak onto DCA property to feed the dogs."

"I do too! I'm telling the truth. And I can prove it! I keep the treats hidden in an old barrel behind the kennel, where Ms. Daniels grows flowers."

"In a barrel." Sarcasm and disbelief practically dripped from Macon's words.

"Yes, sir. Right outside the back door of the kennel building."

Macon muttered beneath his breath. "Brady, I hate to ask—"

"I'm on it. I'll radio Cal and Dillon to let them know I'm heading out to the kennel building."

Brady hurried outside, his boots echoing on the stairs.

"Kyle, if you really saw someone else—"

"I did. Cross my heart, hope to die."

"If you saw someone, do you think you could work with a sketch artist to come up with a picture of him?"

He shrugged. "I dunno. Maybe. It was dark. But there are lights out by the kennels, and the training ring. I caught a glimpse of his face here and there. He was tall. That I remember."

"As tall as me?"

He chuckled. "Dude. You're like the tallest cop in the police department. Nah, shorter than you. But not by a whole lot. Maybe three or four inches."

"So, about six feet tall?"

"Or a little under. Yeah, seems about right. Skinny,

too. White guy. That I'm sure of. He was real pale under the lights."

Macon's cell phone buzzed. "You're on speaker. Go ahead, Cal."

"We found a trail. It leads from the back deck of Emma's house, past the outbuildings, and into the trees. Comparing those shoe prints to the ones out where you tackled Kyle, I'd say they're different. The kid was right. Someone else was out here tonight, but they appear to be long gone."

Macon sighed and scrubbed the stubble on his chin. "Thanks, Cal." He ended the call.

The phone immediately buzzed again. "You're on speaker, Brady. Let us have it."

"I dug around in the barrel. There's a whole bunch of purple and white flowers. And one enormous bag of dog jerky, Meaty Bones and rawhide chews."

Macon shook his head in defeat. "Understood. Thanks, Brady."

"Should I bring the dog treats back to the house?"

"I don't give a flying—"

"Yes, please," Emma interrupted, trying not to laugh. "Some of the dogs really are on special diets. I give them treats, but I have to dole out specific ones to each dog."

"Will do."

Macon pitched his phone onto the side table and stood.

"On your feet, Kyle."

Kyle's eyes widened. "You're still arresting me? For feeding the dogs?"

"No, Kyle. I'm not arresting you for feeding the dogs."

Emma hurried to the couch just as Macon jerked Kyle up and turned him around. Her words of protest died unsaid as Macon unlocked Kyle's handcuffs.

Chapter Seventeen

Emma sipped her coffee, marveling at how beautiful the mountains looked through the kitchen back door. Living in Idaho was a nature lover's dream, with beauty around every corner. She loved everything about it. From the local festivals where everyone gorged on potatoes cooked a dozen different ways, drenched in fry sauce of course, to white water rafting down any of a dozen waterways just outside of Jasper.

Normally, on a gorgeous weekend like this one, she'd feed and water the animals since Piper and Barbara weren't here on weekends. After that, if the weather was this sunny, she'd be grabbing her backpack and hiking into the foothills. Or maybe she'd rent a canoe and enjoy a ride down the Salmon River. But those carefree days were over, at least for now. She had no intention of taking Angel on a raft or hiking in the mountains.

Of course, both Barbara and Piper had offered to help her on weekends because of Angel. But Emma had bought a baby monitor and assured them she would only go outside to do chores when Angel was sleeping. And she'd lock the house up tight. She also wouldn't be gone for more than a few minutes at a time, just to make certain the baby was safe. It would make her chores take a lot longer that way, but it was worth it to make sure that Angel was okay. Of course, she really didn't have to worry today since Macon had spent the night. She and the baby were both safe with him watching over them. All she really needed to worry about was keeping warm. Today had dawned chilly, almost cold, much like the morning Angel had been left on her doorstep.

Taking one last sip from her nearly empty coffee cup, she rinsed it and set it in the sink. Time to get Angel up and change and feed her. Once she was down for a nap, Emma would put the baby monitor receiver in her pocket and go feed the animals. If she didn't do that soon, the dogs would start barking and Presley would be kicking his stall down to get into the pasture.

It was surprising that Angel had slept this late. Normally she'd wake Emma at dawn, crying because of a wet diaper, or hungry for her bottle. It was a blessing that she hadn't this morning, because Emma had been exhausted after everything that had happened last night.

She'd taken advantage of Angel's late morning by taking a quick shower and enjoying a cup of coffee.

But now she was starting to get worried. Angel had never slept this late before.

She headed down the hallway, passing Macon's closed door. He was sleeping late, too, for which she was also grateful. He'd still been awake when she'd gone to bed at midnight. The sleep would do him good.

When she opened the door to Angel's room, she stopped in surprise. Macon wasn't in the guest room. He was right here, in the rocking chair, cradling the baby against his chest as both of them slept.

The sight of big, powerful Macon so sweetly holding delicate little Angel had her heart going all gooey and warm. As she watched, the baby stirred, making happy gurgling sounds. Macon instinctively cuddled her closer, gently patting her back. Angel settled down, smacking her little mouth content-edly, and Macon's breaths resumed their deep, even sounds. He hadn't even woken up, and yet he'd auto-matically soothed the baby and held her protectively. Even Bogie, curled up on the floor, merely blinked his eyes at the interruption, then settled back down to sleep.

Emma pressed her hand to her chest as she watched them. It was such a beautiful sight, the quintessential perfect little family. A strong, hand-some father who only used that strength to help others. The beautiful daughter whose innocence and happiness were jealously guarded and cherished. The family dog, curled up and protective of both of them.

And the mother, watching it all, her heart near to bursting with joy at the wondrousness of it.

Of course, the Norman Rockwell fantasy wasn't reality. Emma wasn't a mother. Macon wasn't her husband or a father. And Angel was only here until her true parents could be found. Emma would do well to remember that. But the fantasy, as brief as it was, had touched her deeply and had her wondering whether she was wrong to resist her fierce attraction to Macon. And whether maybe the possibility of love, and a real family, was worth the risk of being hurt.

Was it? Worth the risk? Was this what she wanted out of life? Someone like Macon to hold her, to love her every day? A child they'd made together? There was no sense in denying that the idea felt wonderful. But was she really willing to risk allowing herself to love again, especially a policeman, knowing that knock could come on the door one night as it had for her mother, telling her that her husband was dead? She didn't know if she could even survive that kind of loss again, though the idea of a future with Macon had every nerve in her body singing and crying out, *go for it!*

The ringing of the doorbell shook her out of her thoughts. Macon's eyes flew open and his gaze locked onto her. His mouth curved in a smile that had her heart fluttering again.

"Morning," he said.

"Morning." Her voice came out a dry rasp. She

cleared her throat. "Someone's at the door. I'll go see who it is."

He was shaking his head before she even finished talking. "I'll get the door. You stay here until I know it's safe." He stood and passed the baby to her, then hurried down the hall.

Emma changed Angel's diaper, then dressed her in a onesie with feet in it to keep her warm.

Footsteps sounded down the hall. Emma turned with the baby in her arms as Macon entered the room. She was just about to ask him who was at the door when he stepped back to let someone else in.

The smile Emma had for Macon faded as she recognized their early-morning surprise visitor. It was Mr. Burns, the caseworker from the Department of Child and Family Services.

MACON HAD HELPED Emma feed the animals or they wouldn't have made it to the police station this quickly, especially since she'd also had to pack a diaper bag for Angel and make up some bottles of formula. Emma was still fighting to hold back tears when he pulled the SUV into a parking spot.

She unclipped her seat belt. "I still can't believe DCF is allowed to show up like that and just steal her."

"He didn't steal her. He took her to a doctor for a routine checkup. You should know more than most that popping in unexpectedly like that is something DCF does on purpose, to catch the fosters off guard.

They want to make sure the baby was being well cared for by surprising you. He certainly didn't have any complaints. And it worked out great anyway since our guys need to search your property for evidence from last night's happenings at your place. You won't have to be there while they're running around and you can attend this morning's status meeting. It's a win-win.

"Chief Walters has been asking me to bring you to one of our meetings so you could review some of the background information we've gathered. I just haven't had time to arrange it. Everything worked out for the best with Mr. Burns stopping by unexpectedly. You don't need to worry about Angel. Burns will call me when he's done and we'll pick her up, or have her brought here."

"It still seems fishy to me. What doctor works on Sundays?"

"The kind that works in a hospital. Mr. Burns said the doctor has a contract with DCF, so that's where he took her."

"I don't like it. Angel doesn't know him. She could be scared right now, wondering what's going on."

Macon gave her a droll look. "She was giggling when he strapped her into the car seat."

"She's too young to giggle. It was gas."

He laughed. "Probably so. I appreciate that you're okay not being at your place while our team looks for evidence. A lot of people wouldn't consent to let us comb over everything when they weren't home."

"Jasper PD is like family to me. I'm not worried about them being out there unsupervised. And Jason's familiar with how I run things and where everything is. He can also help with the animals if something comes up."

"Jason." He practically spat the name. "I still need to talk to him about his failure to keep you safe. He shouldn't have left before I got there."

She put her hand on his. "No, you don't need to talk to him. Trust me, he feels awful and it won't happen again. He was eager to gain your trust again this morning by watching over things."

"He told you that?"

"I inferred it."

He laughed. "I'm still going to talk to him. Eventually. When I'm less angry." He checked the time on his phone. "Kyle and his parents should be here by now. I'll take you to the break room to wait while I speak to them. Then we'll head into the chief's meeting."

They both got out and headed toward the front doors.

"Why are you meeting with Kyle's parents?"

"I need them to sign a consent form so Kyle can work with the sketch artist this morning." He held one of the double doors open for her.

"Mind if I join you? I might be able to help smooth things over. You aren't exactly their favorite person right now."

"Tell me about it. When I drove Kyle home last night, his mother was so mad she wouldn't even talk to me. His father wasn't home, so I didn't get a chance to explain things to him. No telling what version of the story Kyle gave them after I left."

"They're good people. I think they mean well."

"They acted willing to cooperate when you and I went there, but since then, they've done the complete opposite. They lied for him, covered for him every time I tried to find him to ask him more questions."

"They love him and they were protecting him. Let's just get this over with."

Twenty minutes later, Kyle was working with a sketch artist and his parents had apologized repeatedly to Macon over their earlier behavior. It wasn't because of Emma's skills in getting them to calm down, either. It was because Macon had gotten impatient and told them that if they'd made Kyle talk to him instead of covering for him and allowing him to hide out, Macon may not have jumped to the wrong conclusions last night and nearly put Kyle in jail. That realization had them both sputtering. They couldn't sign the consent papers fast enough.

Macon led Emma into the main conference room where the chief, Rutledge, Cal and a few others were discussing all the happenings at DCA. Pens, bright yellow legal pads and folders were scattered around the table. A whiteboard hanging on the far wall displayed a smattering of pictures, including one of Angel and what appeared to be a satellite image of Emma's property showing the various buildings. She was a little disappointed there weren't red strings attaching everything in a spiderweb pattern like she'd seen on TV crime dramas. But she'd learned long ago from her father that real police work wasn't nearly as flashy as those television shows would have you believe.

Emma hadn't been sitting for more than a minute before Rutledge stood, giving her an annoyed look.

"I've seen what I needed to see for now. I'm not going to waste any more time discussing a K-9 training facility. Cal, if something useful to the investigation comes up, let me know."

Macon squeezed Emma's hand reassuringly beneath the table as Rutledge left the room.

She put on a brave face and smiled as if it hadn't bothered her. But she couldn't help being annoyed by his attitude. She also couldn't help wondering if there may be something more behind his dislike of all things DCA related. For a man who professed that he despised her program, he'd seemingly gone out of his way to show up at her property recently. Was he keeping tabs on her for some reason? Could he be the one behind everything going on? While she couldn't see him as someone who'd kidnap or abandon a baby on her doorstep, she couldn't as easily dismiss the idea of him causing problems at her ranch. Maybe he was trying to harass her, scare her, to get her to close it down?

Macon spread out a group of folders in the middle of the table as he answered a question from the chief.

Emma glanced at the stack and immediately recognized the name on one of the tabs, Maria Loretto. She'd been on the list of foster kids he'd shown her yesterday. Did the entire folder contain information about her?

She leaned slightly forward to read some of the other folder tabs. She barely refrained from rolling her eyes when she saw folders for William, Hugh and Kyle. But there were many others she and Macon had discussed last night, including David Timmons, Kelvin Armstrong, Josh Basham and Wanda Mickelson. There was even one on Celia Banks, which seemed like a complete waste of time. Emma had marked her name with an *L* the other day for low priority. But that was the folder Macon reached for now.

As he browsed through it, the chief aimed a fatherly smile at Emma. "Thanks for coming to the meeting. Macon told me you gave him some insight about some of the people he's been investigating. When he and I spoke this morning, he relayed what you'd said about high and low priority potential suspects. So I had Cal here organize the folders along those lines and update them with recent interview sheets or pictures we've been collecting. As a result, he discovered something I felt that both you and Macon needed to see right away." He waved toward Macon. "From the look on Macon's face, I'm guessing he's seen what Cal pointed out to me. Go ahead. Show her."

Macon pulled two pictures from the folder and

set one on the table in front of Emma. "That's what Celia Banks looks like today."

Emma nodded, smiling at the pretty dark-haired, dark-eyed girl she remembered so fondly. She hadn't changed much in the handful of years since Emma had last seen her.

"And this," Macon said, as he placed another picture on top of the first, "is what she looked like when she was a baby."

Emma froze, stunned as she stared at the photograph. If Macon hadn't told her it was Celia, she'd have sworn her last nickel that it was a picture of Angel.

Chapter Eighteen

"What happens now?" Emma was unable to keep her voice from shaking. "Obviously Angel is Celia's baby. Is DCF going to take her away?" Her face grew warm at the looks of sympathy aimed her way. There was no point in pretending she wasn't devastated over the prospect of giving up the baby. As hard as she'd tried not to, she'd grown to love her. And she was silently cursing herself for letting her heart get involved.

Which was another reason she needed to put the brakes on her Rockwell fantasy of Macon and her potentially becoming a family. She couldn't survive having him, then losing him. Her heart was already halfway his and she needed to protect herself from becoming even more entangled.

Macon reached for her hand again beneath the table and squeezed it as if to reassure her. She tugged her hand loose, her heart breaking just a little more at the surprised look on his face.

He crossed his forearms on top of the table. "That's not how it works. No one's taking Angel just yet. We'll interview Celia, find out what's going on and whether she says Angel is hers or denies it. Either way, a blood sample will be drawn so a lab can test it and prove whether she's Angel's mother."

"She is," Emma insisted. "Everyone in this room knows it. That picture is proof."

"A judge won't see it that way," Macon continued. "He'll want the blood test. But DCF is the legal guardian right now. They won't wait for the blood test results. They'll start investigating Celia right now, with the assumption that she's the mother to save time. Their goal will be to find out whether she's a fit parent. The answer to that seems like an obvious no. A fit parent would have reported their child missing, or wouldn't have abandoned her if Celia is the one who did that. If she hopes to regain custody, she'll likely have to jump through a ton of hoops to convince DCF and a judge that she'll make better decisions for her daughter here on out."

Emma glanced at him, hope flaring inside her. But as soon as it did, guilt slammed down hard. She shouldn't be rooting for a woman to fail DCF's tests so that Emma could keep her daughter a little longer. That was awful, especially given that Emma knew Celia, or had at one time. Something terrible must have happened to make her give up Angel. Or maybe someone had stolen her and Celia, for some unknown reason, was too afraid to report it. Either way, Celia would need Emma's support going forward. Not her jealousy and resentment.

She drew a bracing breath and forced a smile. "Celia is a good person. I'm sure there's a reasonable explanation, at least in her mind, as to why Angel ended up at my door. And I can't imagine, given the chance, that Celia wouldn't do everything she can to get her daughter back. We need to help her."

"First things first." Macon pulled a business card out of his wallet and slid it across the table toward Dillon. "That's the DCF caseworker's card. Mr. Burns has Angel at the hospital seeing a pediatrician right now for a checkup. Would you mind telling him our suspicions? He can start an investigation on his end and order the blood test to prove whether or not Angel is Celia's baby while the baby is already at the hospital."

"No problem." Dillon took the card and left the room.

Macon grabbed a pen and legal pad from the middle of the table. "Emma, if you want to help Celia, then start by telling us everything you remember about her, not just the quick summary you gave me last night."

"I didn't actually foster her very long. She was seventeen when she came to live with me." Emma proceeded to tell them about the shy, sweet teenager who'd been left an orphan after her parents died in a car accident. Her only relatives were some aging grandparents with health issues. They were unwilling and unable to raise their granddaughter. And since they lived on the other side of the country,

Celia had rarely seen them and barely even knew them. Foster care had been her only option until she turned eighteen and could live on her own.

"I helped her with her studies, showed her the ropes at DCA. But she was far more interested in boys than studying or helping with the animals. She got in trouble for skipping school quite a few times, always to hang out with some guy. But she always felt guilty later and made up for it. She got good grades, aced most of her tests. Still, with so many unexcused absences she was in danger of failing. I tried everything I could to help her graduate. But when her latest boyfriend came along, it was basically over. She failed twelfth grade and, as far as I know, never did go back and finish. A month later, she turned eighteen and aged out of foster care." She held her hands up in a helpless gesture. "I offered for her to stay with me but all she wanted was to go off with Sean. I haven't seen or heard about her since."

The chief leaned forward in his chair at the head of the rectangular table. "Wasn't there a Sean on that high priority list you discussed with Macon?"

"Sean Hopper, yes. That's the boy she fell the hardest for. He was several years older than her, working odd jobs to get by. He was cute and seemed cool to a girl like Celia. She didn't look much deeper than that. He was the resident bad boy, but not just by reputation. He really was bad. He'd been in trouble with the law for petty crimes for years. I imagine by now he's done some time in jail, maybe even prison. That's really all I can tell you. That folder has a lot of pieces of paper in it. You probably know a lot more than I've ever known about Celia and her old boyfriends."

Macon leaned forward. "A few things, nothing substantial. Until I saw that baby picture of Celia, I wasn't seriously considering her as the possible mother to Angel. But now we'll dig, hard, into both her background and, as you said, any guys she hangs with or once hung with. I do have a local address, so that will make it easier."

"When are you going to talk to her?" she asked.

He pushed his chair back. "I'm going to head over there right now. Given the circumstances, I'd rather surprise her and not give her a chance to make up a false story or go into hiding. I'll drop you off at your place on the way."

"No need." She pushed her own chair back and smiled her thanks at the others around the table. "I've been meaning to visit Jenny for a while. Seems like I haven't talked to her in ages. I can get someone else to take me home later."

Macon frowned. "Jenny Dix? The dispatcher?"

"One and the same. I know she gets a lot of downtime between calls. Or at least, she did before the latest spate of crimes at my place." She laughed nervously, avoiding Macon's questioning gaze as she escaped from the conference room.

Yes, she was a coward, avoiding him this way. But just thinking about losing Angel was splintering her into little pieces. If she allowed herself to spend more time alone with Macon, and fall for him even harder, then when he inevitably left her at some point—whether by choice or chance—it would obliterate what was left of her heart. She had to stop this…thing, this attraction between them, before it was too late.

If it wasn't already.

She'd only made it around the corner from the conference room when a hand grasped her elbow and gently turned her around.

Macon.

"What's wrong, Emma? What did I do to make you upset with me?"

Her heart cracked a little more. It was the hardest thing she'd ever done to stand there and force a confused look on her face.

And lie.

"I don't know what you mean, Macon. Everything's good. Looks like you may have solved the most important issue—finding Angel's mom. I agree with your theory that Angel is connected to the other events on my property. So you should be able to figure out who's behind it all in a matter of days, maybe even today. It's a relief. You won't have to come guard me anymore. Bogie is doing great and doesn't need additional training. It's been great seeing you again after all this time, but now we can each go back to our normal lives. Neither of us will have to see each other every day. We're free."

She forced herself to smile up at him in spite of the hurt and confusion in his gaze.

"Free? We can both go back to our separate lives, the way they were before all this? That's what you want?"

She frowned. "Well, of course. Don't you?"

He stood there for a long moment. Then his expression smoothed out, becoming unreadable. He gave her a curt nod. "I'll call you later with an update on the case. Jason's watching your place right now. I'll get someone else to cover the night shift instead of me since that appears to be your preference. If you wanted to be free of me, Emma, all you had to do was tell me. I'm not the kind of man who would ever force his presence on someone who doesn't want him." He turned around and strode back to the conference room.

As soon as the door closed behind him, the first sob hit. She covered her mouth and sprinted for the bathroom so she could fall apart in private.

Chapter Nineteen

Barbara leaned across the kitchen table and put her hand on top of Emma's. "Quit thanking me for coming over. That's what friends are for. My weekends aren't sacred. Goodness, I'm alone most of the time anyway. Samantha's away at college right now. And Bob would much rather go off with his buddies fishing than watch me work in my garden." She patted Emma's hand and sat back. "What you need to do is quit crying about Angel. She's not going anywhere, not right now anyway. That's what Macon said, right? These things take time."

Emma went along with Barbara's assumption that it was just Angel who had her upset. Macon was as much on her mind, and her heart, as the baby and accounted for at least half her tears. Emma felt awful for how she'd had to leave things with him. It was tearing her apart, even though she knew it was for the best. She just wished it didn't hurt so much.

"I know, I know," Emma said. "But even with

her off with that Mr. Burns the house feels way too empty."

Jason leaned over from where he was sitting on the couch, watching TV. "I don't count? Is that it?" He grinned.

Barbara gave him an admonishing look. "Shouldn't you be making rounds or something? Making sure no one's sneaking around the place?"

He chuckled and stood. "I can take a hint. I need to stretch my legs anyway."

"Sorry, Jason," Emma called out.

"No worries. Be back soon."

"Not too soon I hope," Barbara called after him as he shut the front door.

"You're so bad." Emma smiled.

"Nah, I've known Jason almost as long as you have. He gets me. And it was worth picking on him to see you smile again. What time are you expecting that family services guy to bring Angel back?"

"That's just it. I have no idea. This morning I thought it would be for a couple of hours. But it's late afternoon now and I haven't heard from Mr. Burns or anyone else. I don't know what's going on. I'm guessing the discovery that Celia is likely the mother changed everything."

"Macon hasn't called with any updates?"

She briefly closed her eyes. "Things were, ah, difficult at the station between us. He's probably giving me my space, hoping I snap out of it and go back to normal."

"You really care about him, don't you?"

Emma stared at her in surprise. "It's that obvious?"

Barbara laughed. "Are you kidding? Honey, it was obvious a couple of years ago when you were training him and that dog of his. I'm just surprised it took you this long to realize it."

She dropped her head in her hands. "What am I going to do? This is a disaster."

"Why? It's obvious he cares about you, too."

"You don't understand."

"Which is why I'm asking."

Emma sighed and sat back.

Barbara dunked a fry into the homemade fry sauce that Emma had made to thank her for coming over. After chasing it down with a sip of iced tea, she said, "Enlighten me. Because we both know you didn't ask me over here just because of what's going on with Angel. You're hurting, bad. And Macon is at the center of it."

"You're wrong. I hadn't planned on talking about him at all. I really did call you because I wanted to commiserate about the baby."

"Well, I'm not leaving until you spill the beans on why it's such a bad thing that you and Macon are obviously wild about each other. To my knowledge, other than that Billy guy who nearly destroyed your life during your rebellious phase—"

"Ugh. Please don't mention Billy."

"Just sayin', other than him, you've never let any

other guys into your life that I know of. You deserve some fun, Emma. And if I read things right, Macon's a dang good one, a keeper. Talk to me. Bob won't be back from his fishing trip until tomorrow afternoon. I've got all night." She popped another drenched fry into her mouth.

Emma let out a shaky breath. "That's just it. Other than...the bad phase in my life, there's been no one. By choice. I've lost so many people I've loved and been hurt by the very people who were supposed to love me the most. The one time I took a chance was he who shall not be named again, and that nearly led to me going to prison. It took years for me to build a life, to create the Daniels Canine Academy, to learn to be happy again. I know Macon is a good man, the best. He'd never hurt me on purpose. But if I give him what's left of my heart, and he either moves back to Boise or something happened to him, I don't think I could survive."

"Oh, sweetie. Don't you see? You've already given him your heart. And you can't live your life trying to avoid pain. It's just not possible. And really, is that even a life, one without love? You remember how much you loved your siblings, and then your parents—Rick and Susan Daniels. And you're scared because you don't want to hurt the way you did when you lost them. But would you have rather never known your siblings? Never been taken in by Rick and Susan? Would your life really have been better if you'd never loved at all? The whole point of life is to share it with people you care about. And, heck, no way would Macon move off and leave you, not if you give him a chance to break past that wall of yours."

She squeezed Emma's hand again. "Love is a rare and precious gift. Not everyone gets a chance at it. You've got that chance right in front of you. What you have to ask yourself is whether you'd rather spend the rest of your life knowing you threw that chance away. I can tell you right now, if Bob died tomorrow it would be the hardest thing I've ever faced. But I wouldn't undo all our years together to avoid that pain. I cherish every moment we've had together. What's that cliché? Better to have loved and lost than to never have loved? It's true, Emma. It's so true."

Emma stared at her in dismay as her words sank in. "Even if you're right, it doesn't matter. I hurt him. And there's no way he'll ever be able to forgive what I did." She burst into tears.

Chapter Twenty

Riding her horses had always been Emma's favorite escape when she was stressed out, even more so than working with her beloved K-9s. And with the mess that her life had become, the only exercise Presley and Elton had gotten lately was when she let them out in the pasture on their own. So after convincing Barbara that she'd be all right and it was okay to leave, Emma had headed out to the barn.

Jason wasn't too happy about her decision since he felt compelled to sit with Bogie against the fence that circled the pasture to keep an eye on her. He was an excellent horseman, having helped her with Presley and Elton when he'd been a foster here. But he wanted to be able to scan their surroundings while she was outside to make sure no one sneaked up on them. Doing that on top of a trotting horse was a recipe for disaster. Plus, Bogie could be a problem if they were both on horses. He might get underfoot. So Jason was relegated to looking around and

whiling away his time with the shepherd while also
keeping an eye on her.

But Emma didn't mind being alone, or relatively
alone. She was sick to death of being babysat and had
told him he could wait for her up at the house rather
than out here. His insistence on watching her while
she trotted Presley around the pasture was his decision. And she desperately needed this mindless exercise to try to come to terms with everything that
was going on and pull herself together.

The names of everyone she'd loved and lost beat
a mournful drum in her mind in rhythm with Presley's hooves.

Danny.

Little Katie.

Her biological mom and dad—before drugs and
alcohol had turned them into monsters.

Rick Daniels.

Susan Daniels.

Countless fosters who'd broken her heart each and
every time one of them left. At least with them, it
wasn't the grief of complete loss like it had been for
her loved ones who'd passed away. But it was still
difficult, and there was only so much sorrow one person could bear. She'd vowed never to risk her heart
like that again. She didn't really count bad boy Billy.
That wasn't love. It was rebellion. There'd been no
one else in her heart for so long.

Then Macon had shown up.

He was so handsome, charming. So fun to laugh

with while she'd trained him and Bogie several years ago. She'd loosened up, enjoyed him, allowed herself to have fun knowing she'd never see him again. She'd reasoned that he was a "safe" man to flirt with because he'd return to Boise and that was that. But then he'd come back to Jasper, and the feelings she'd thought she'd buried so long ago had exploded to the surface.

Macon and Angel. She loved both of them. There was no point in denying it now. And she was losing both of them. Just as she'd feared, it was tearing her apart. She knew Barbara was right, that love was really what made life worth living. Because her world had been gray, safe, before Macon and Angel had reawakened her to the wonderful colors all around her. How was she supposed to go back to life the way it had been now that she knew what she was missing?

Presley stumbled on the turn at the far end of the pasture. She eased up on the reins and patted his neck. She hadn't been paying attention and had been holding the reins too tightly, interfering with his gait and his ability to stretch out for the turn. Stupid, stupid. She could have caused him to break a leg and he'd have had to be put down. There was nothing more dangerous while riding a horse than to not be paying attention.

"I'm sorry, boy." She patted his neck again. "Goodness, you're all lathered up. Too much exercise after being cooped up so much, isn't that right?

Come on. I'll give you extra oats for supper to make it up to you."

He whinnied as if he understood as she turned him toward the barn.

Jason caught her attention at the fence, motioning to her. Bogie was standing at attention as well. She looked past them and saw why. Two cars were coming up the driveway. One was a Jasper PD SUV. The other was a car she remembered from when she'd transferred the car seat from it to Macon's vehicle at the hospital. It belonged to Mr. Burns, the Child and Family Services caseworker.

She dismounted as Jason and Bogie joined her outside the barn.

"Who is it?" she asked, both dreading and hoping that Macon was in the SUV.

"I don't know. No one called to say they were coming." He sounded irritated about that fact.

Together they watched as Mr. Burns's car turned up the circular drive, disappearing when the house blocked their view. The SUV continued toward them, parking several yards away, probably so they wouldn't spook the horse or risk hitting Bogie. This close, even with the windows being darkly tinted, she could see who was driving. And the way Bogie was standing at attention, he knew, too.

Macon.

Seeing him again, so soon after their disastrous morning, and her falling apart in her kitchen after realizing she was in love with him, had her pulse rushing in her ears. But when both passenger doors opened and the chief and office manager, Theresa, stepped out, her trepidation turned to alarm.

"What's happened?" she demanded as they all moved toward her and Jason. "Is Angel okay? I saw Mr. Burns drive up to the house—"

"She's fine," Macon assured her, his voice gentle and soothing even though she didn't deserve for him to treat her so kindly. "Angel did great at her checkup, got a clean bill of health. And she had the blood test too. The doctor said she's thriving under your care. Mr. Burns brought her back. She's up at the house with him." He patted Bogie, who'd ducked under the fence rail to sit in the gravel beside him.

Relief had Emma pressing a shaky hand to her chest. "Thank goodness she's okay. Thank you, Macon."

He nodded, his smile fading as he gestured to the chief. "I asked Chief Walters to come with me to update you on the latest happenings."

The rest of his words went unsaid, but she understood his meaning. It was his case. He wanted to update her and answer her questions. But he'd brought the chief along to keep things on a more formal, less personal basis.

She really hated herself right now.

"And Theresa? You're always welcome here, but I'm wondering why you came. You rarely make the trip out this way."

Theresa smiled. "Macon will explain."

Jason took Presley's reins. "Ms. Daniels, how about I rub Presley down and get both of the horses settled for the night while y'all talk this out."

She smiled her gratitude and stepped through the gate to join the others.

"We found Celia Banks fairly easily," Macon told her. "The chief went with me since she's met him before. We thought it might put her more at ease. It didn't. She was really nervous, burst into tears the second we drove up. She didn't even try to deny the truth. She's the one who left Angel on your porch. And Angel is her child, only her real name is Anna."

Emma's stomach dropped as if she was on a roller coaster. "I guess the DNA test isn't necessary after all."

"Oh, it's necessary. It's required, actually. The chief secured a court order even before we got to Celia's place to compel her to provide a DNA sample. It's being driven to the state lab as we speak, along with a sample taken from the baby when she was at the hospital. The chief pulled some strings to put a rush on it. But it will still take longer than we'd like. We still don't have the DNA results back from the other sample we sent, from those shrubs by your porch. As to Angel, I mean Anna, Celia had pictures of her, as you'd expect. And DCF used the footprints on her birth certificate as a preliminary way to verify her identity. The prints match."

"No surprise there, but now I'm confused. Is… Anna…staying with me now or going back to Celia?"

The chief patted her shoulder as if she were his daughter. "For now, you're still watching little Anna. DCF trusts you to keep her safe until Celia can prove to the court that she's a fit mother. Right now, she's not, obviously, after having left her baby on someone's porch. But there *are* extenuating circumstances that are being taken into account. She'll have to take some parenting courses, maintain employment and do a host of other things in order to get Anna back. It could be months or longer before DCF recommends a hearing to transfer custody to her."

Emma struggled to take it all in, make sense of what they were saying. Everything was happening so quickly.

"Emma," Macon asked, "are you okay watching over the baby for that long? Especially knowing that you'll have to give her up if Celia is granted custody again?"

"Oh, yes," she said, without hesitation. And she realized it was true. She smiled. "I love Angel. I mean Anna. Wow, that's going to be hard to get used to, a new name. I love her and enjoy taking care of her. But what's most important is that we do what's best for her. I'll enjoy keeping her until her mom can take over."

Macon smiled. "If you weren't okay with that, Theresa had volunteered to take Anna until Mr. Burns could find another foster situation. They're still short on families in the area willing and able to take in babies."

Emma hugged Theresa. "That's so sweet of you. I really appreciate it. And now I know who to ask to babysit if I ever need a night off," she teased.

Theresa hugged her fiercely and stepped back, her eyes suspiciously misty. "My Henry and I, God rest his soul, were never blessed with children. I'd love to watch Anna for you any time."

The chief smiled, too, and patted Theresa's back. Then, as if suddenly realizing what he was doing, he dropped his hand and awkwardly cleared his throat.

Emma thought it was sweet that, once again, the chief and Theresa were trying to keep their relationship a secret. She glanced at Macon, who was watching her intently, as if trying to figure her out.

She nervously smoothed her hands down her jeans. "Did Celia tell you the name of Anna's father? I'd think he'd be given custody instead of leaving her with me, unless he has to go through everything Celia will to be deemed a fit parent too?"

Macon leaned against the wooden fence. "The father is her boyfriend, Sean Hopper, the same guy you remembered being a bad influence on her years ago."

Emma nodded, not really surprised, but sad too. She'd hoped for so much better for sweet Celia.

"They'll do a paternity test to confirm that Sean is the father, but there's no reason to doubt it. And, if everything Celia told us about Sean is true," Macon continued, "Sean is the reason she left Anna here. She was afraid of him, afraid he'd hurt her. Celia's life post–foster care has been rough. Sean is a small-time criminal and has been abusing Celia. She thought, mistakenly, that having a baby would calm him down, make him want to be better. Instead, the violence escalated after Anna was born and their financial struggles got worse. But until recently, he'd never hit Anna."

Emma pressed a hand to her mouth, afraid of what else he was going to say.

"He never hit the baby," he reassured her, his voice gentle again. "But he tried. When he went to punch her, Celia threw herself between them and took the beating instead. After that, she knew she had to leave. She couldn't risk Anna being hurt. But she didn't have money or a job. She was desperate. And she didn't trust the cops or anyone else, except you. She told me you're the only person after her parents' deaths who ever genuinely cared about her. Leaving Anna here, to her, wasn't abandonment. It was a second chance."

"Poor Celia," Emma whispered. "What happened to her after that? You said she didn't have a job or money."

"We found her in a women's shelter one county over. But since I found her so easily, I figure her boyfriend can also find her, if he's looking. So I took her with me when I left. She's at the station right now." He motioned to Theresa. "Theresa's going to pick her up after we leave and take Celia to her place."

"And I'll help her get back on her feet," Theresa added. "She certainly won't go hungry. And we'll try to find her a job. Of course, she'll have to delay starting one until Sean is found."

Emma shook her head. "She was such a good kid. I hate that she's mixed up with him. But she'll be okay. Theresa will make sure of it." She smiled her thanks again.

The chief nodded, as if in agreement that Theresa would take care of Celia. "I'll stop by and check on her after work every day." He cleared his throat. "To check on Celia. Just in case Sean is trying to find her. She's tried to leave him before and he always hunted her down and forced her to come back. Worried he'd do that again, she's been moving from shelter to shelter to keep a step ahead of him."

"And left Anna with me so she wouldn't be in danger." She glanced back and forth between the chief and Macon. "But it sounds like he must have figured out that Anna was here and has been sneaking around, trying to break in, cause me problems. Is that the going theory?"

Macon shifted against the fence. "It makes the most sense, when taking everything else into account. None of our other potential suspects have panned out. And the trouble here at DCA didn't start until Celia left Anna with you. When we asked her if she thought Sean would harass you if he thought you had Anna, she said that's exactly the kind of thing he'd do. He might not want Anna, but he wouldn't want someone else to have her, either. That's the kind of abusive, controlling person he is. If your alarm hadn't gone off that night when he broke in and scared him away, there's no telling what he might have done."

She shivered and wrapped her arms around her waist.

He moved closer, as if wanting to put his arm around her, but stopped, his expression hardening.

Grief and guilt—for what she'd done, for how she'd treated him—had her fighting back tears. How could she ever make this right? She swiped at her eyes. This wasn't the time to think about that. She needed to get to Anna, make sure she was okay. Feed her, give her a bath. There was so much to do when taking care of a little baby. And she looked forward to every minute she had left with her.

The chief motioned to Macon. "Show her the pictures."

"Oh, forgot about that."

"Pictures?" Emma asked.

Macon tapped his phone screen, then turned it around, revealing a typical police mugshot. "Recognize him?"

She frowned and moved closer. "No…wait. The eyes are the same, but it's been a few years. Is that Sean?"

He nodded and flipped to another photo before holding up his phone again. "Recognize this guy?"

"Well, of course. That's Sean, too. Why?"

He put his phone away. "That's the rendering the artist drew based on Kyle's eyewitness statements about the man he saw the night the dogs were let out.

I sent a photo lineup to Kyle. He picked Sean out right away."

"That's great. I guess we can take Captain Rutledge off the suspect list now, huh?"

Macon's eyes widened.

"Rutledge?" The chief looked confused. "Arthur was on your suspect list?"

"No," Macon said.

"Yes," Emma said.

Macon rolled his eyes.

Emma relaxed, relief easing the tension in her shoulders. "Then it's over, really over, right, Macon? Celia is Anna's mom. And Sean is the one who's been trying to scare me, or worse."

"We know who, and have a guess as to why. But it's not over until Sean's locked up. We sent a team to arrest him but he wasn't home. His neighbors told us he's usually home this time of day, boozing it up with whatever money he made working. He might have seen the cop cars and got spooked. We've got a BOLO out on him and in the neighboring counties so law enforcement will be on the lookout both for him and his car. But until he's behind bars you're still in danger."

She muttered beneath her breath and leaned against the fence. "I'm still going to have a babysitter."

His mouth twitched as if he wanted to smile, but he held it back. "An officer needs to be here at DCA until Sean is put away, yes."

Jason stepped out of the barn as Macon was talking and joined them on the other side of the fence. "What did I miss?"

"Too much to repeat right now," Macon told him.

The sound of a car engine had all of them looking toward the driveway. Yet another police SUV rounded the circular drive and disappeared from sight when the house blocked the view.

"What's going on now?" Emma asked, exasperated at the thought of yet another emergency to deal with.

"I can answer that one." Jason waved his hand, smiling. "It's Dillon. He's taking night-shift duties today. He'll have Bentley with him, his Australian shepherd mix, so Bogie can head home with Macon. And, for once, I get to go home on time to my new bride." His grin widened.

Macon narrowed his eyes, making Jason sober. "Remind me to talk to you tomorrow about your duties and how your shift doesn't end until your replacement arrives, no matter how late they might be or who's waiting at home."

Jason swallowed. "Yes, sir. The horses are all set for the night, Ms. Daniels. Need me to do anything else?"

She shook her head. "You've been wonderful, Jason. Thanks so much for taking care of that. Thanks for everything."

"Of course. If you're done here, I'll walk you to the house."

She hesitated and looked at Macon.

"Good idea," Macon told him, even though he was looking at Emma as he spoke. "I'll drive the chief and Theresa to the station. Come, Bogie." He opened the passenger door and Bogie hopped inside. Then he assisted Theresa up into the SUV.

Emma's throat tightened. The chief gave her a sympathetic glance and hugged her.

"It will all work out," he whispered by her ear. "Have faith."

She nodded her thanks, not sure whether the chief was talking about the situation with Sean Hopper, or whether he'd figured out that she was upset about Macon.

"My bride's waiting," Jason teased.

She gave him a wobbly smile and started across the lawn toward the house, while Macon and the others drove away.

Chapter Twenty-One

Emma turned her pickup out of her driveway onto Elm Street. "Thanks for going with me to the feed store, Jason. With all the excitement lately, Barbara and I both forgot to put in our usual order for delivery and are about to run out of dog food."

He gave her a droll look. "Like I'd let you go anywhere without me by your side when it's my turn to guard you. Macon would kill me." He grimaced. "He may kill me anyway. I'm not looking forward to that talk he promised today."

She laughed and turned down another road, heading away from the more populated areas of Jasper. "Barbara was excited to get to stay at DCA with Anna instead of coming along. She really missed the baby. It's good to have her back."

"Tashya and I are thinking about having kids."

"What? Already?"

"Well, not right away. But we're talking about it. She's always wanted a big family. I guess I could handle a few if they're like Angel. I mean Anna. She's pretty cool."

"Yes. She is. I hope you and Tashya have a bunch of rug rats and a dozen grandkids."

"Whoa, whoa. You're already making me a grandpa? I only just got married."

She laughed and turned down the long road the feed store was on. This one wasn't paved and was full of potholes. Her truck squeaked and rattled like it was about to fall apart. But she knew better. It had been around for decades and would probably still be around for decades to come.

"Where is this place?" Jason asked, looking out the window. "It's like we're in Timbuktu or something."

"It's in a perfect location for its purposes. You can't see the houses because of all the trees along the road but there's prime pastureland out this way for families with horses and other livestock." She pointed off to the right. "There, Sampson's Feed and Grain. And it's not in Timbuktu."

"Nearly. Well, at least the parking lot is empty. Easier to keep an eye out for that Sean fellow that way. Still, I'm texting Macon the address just so he knows we're not at DCA. I'm not taking any chances with him. I need this job."

Her stomach tightened as she pulled into a parking space an aisle back from the building so no one could park behind them. They'd need the room to load the bags of feed into the bed of the pickup. "You don't really expect Sean to come all the way out here, do you?"

"Naw. Everyone's looking for him. A woman-beating scumbag like him is a coward. He'll lie low somewhere, waiting for the heat to die down."

"I hope they find him soon. I'm tired of looking over my shoulder."

"Don't worry, Ms. Daniels. I'll keep you safe."

"Are you ever going to call me Emma?"

He looked horrified. "You were like a mom to me when I was at DCA. I'd never call you by your first name. And we're too close in age in the grand scheme of things for me to call you mom."

She laughed. "Ms. Daniels it is. Let's get this over with and head back home. I don't want Barbara to usurp me in Anna's affections."

He chuckled and they headed inside.

Even though the store was obviously empty except for the man at the register, Jason made her wait while he checked both of the bathrooms. As he headed up the aisle toward her, she stared at him.

"Did you really just go into the women's bathroom?"

"Of course. That's a perfect place for a wanted man to hide, thinking no one would check."

"Wanted man?" the cashier asked. "Should I be worried?"

Jason shook his head. "If he shows up, I'll take care of him."

Emma smiled at his confidence, but she prayed

he'd never be put to the test. She knew how danger-ous being a cop could be, even in a relatively peace-ful town like Jasper. After all, her father had been gunned down in the line of duty.

She arranged a delivery date for the supplies that she needed that wouldn't fit in the truck. Jason loaded the fifty-pound bags of dog food onto a roll-ing cart and followed her out of the store.

As he loaded them into the back of the truck, she headed around to the driver's side, then froze in shock. While they'd been in the store, someone had spray-painted filthy words across the door in big orange letters. She whirled around, but the parking lot was empty. Their truck was the only vehicle parked out front. Was there an employee lot in the back? It hadn't occurred to her until now. The cashier must have a ve-hicle somewhere. Had Sean, or someone else, parked there too and vandalized her truck?

"Last one." The truck springs creaked as Jason hoisted the bag into the back, then slammed the tail-gate. He headed around to her side, pushing the cart. "Something wrong? What are you looking—" He swore and shoved the cart out of the way. "Get in, get in." He drew his gun and scanned the parking lot and building, as he reached for the police-radio transmitter on his shoulder with his other hand.

"Get in the truck. Now."

His panicked order finally broke through her shock. She hurried to unlock the door, then yanked it open.

A man jumped up from where he'd been lying across the bench seat and aimed a gun at her face. Sean Hopper. She screamed and slammed the door, knocking his gun arm up.

"Jason, gun!"

He whirled around as she dived to the ground, her purse skittering underneath the truck. Two gunshots rang out, deafeningly loud over the top of her head. A look of shock crossed Jason's face. Then he crumpled to the ground, his pistol skittering across the pavement.

Emma sobbed his name even as she ran forward to grab the gun.

Another shot rang out. The bullet whistled past her so close she could feel its heat. She ducked down and ran to the other side of the truck, crouching behind the engine block. She needed to call 911, but her phone was in her purse, which was under the truck somewhere. She leaned down, trying to see where it was.

"You're just making it worse for yourself, you interfering witch," Sean yelled. "Where are you hiding Celia?"

Her purse was too far under the truck to reach, and she was nothing but a target out here. She needed to get away, hide. The store was surrounded by trees, but they weren't close to the building. She'd have to run a good twenty yards to reach them.

Her heart squeezed in her chest as she thought about poor Jason. Where had he been shot? She pictured him lying there, bleeding out. Had he radioed dispatch before Sean surprised them? She didn't think so. Somehow she had to get him help.

The truck bounced on its springs. The door flew open, its rusty hinges squeaking in protest. "I'm comin' for you. Give up now and I'll kill you fast. Make me work for it and I'll teach you a lesson before I kill you."

She had no choice. She couldn't wait here and let Sean kill her. The only way to help Jason was to survive and call the police. She took off, running in a zigzag pattern toward the store.

Bullets whined past her, burying themselves in the weathered siding of the building. She put on another burst of speed and shoved the glass door, slamming it back against the wall. She ran to the first aisle past the door and crouched down behind the metal shelves.

The cashier was nowhere to be seen. He'd probably heard the gunshots and was hiding. She prayed he'd had the sense to call 911. Where was he hiding? Was there a place she could hide, too? The shelves wouldn't offer her any real protection and they certainly wouldn't conceal her location.

No. She couldn't just hide and wait while Jason died out there. She had to call 911 just in case the cashier hadn't. And she needed to let them know to send an ambulance for Jason.

The glass in the front door shattered as another bullet crashed through it.

Emma let out a squeak of surprise, then took off

running again for the back door beneath a neon red sign marked Exit.

The sound of Sean chuckling as he stalked across the wooden walkway out front had her sprinting forward and bursting through the exit door.

"Those bags of feed won't stop a bullet, Ms. Busybody," he called out from inside the store.

The sound of his laughter sent a frisson of fear up Emma's spine. But she wasn't looking for a place to hide now. She couldn't outrun a bullet. She had to fight fire with fire. She needed to go for Jason's gun and either try to operate the police radio on his uniform or find his phone.

Keeping to the side of the building, she moved as quickly and quietly as she could down the wooden walkway that circled the building like a wraparound porch. She didn't want to go too fast or Sean would hear her and know she'd doubled back, rather than run behind the stacks of feed behind the store. She made it down the side of the building, then stopped at the corner. She glanced behind her to make sure he wasn't there, then hurried to the front.

She raced down the steps toward the truck, hurrying to the driver's side. She skidded to a halt on the gravel, again in shock. Jason wasn't there. Neither was his gun. What did that mean? Had Sean thrown his body somewhere?

Cold fear clutched her chest. She was about to run to the back of the truck to look, when the sound of boots running across the wooden walkway had her jumping into the pickup and slamming the door shut. She was reaching for the keys when Sean rounded the outside of the building and stopped by the ruined front doors. He grinned and held up something shiny and shook it, metal flashing in the sunlight, making a jingling sound.

Keys.

Emma grabbed for the steering column where the truck keys should have been. Sure enough, they were gone. A keening moan wheezed out of her clenched teeth. She was trapped.

Sean slowly raised his gun, grinning the whole time.

The ruined front door of the feed store jerked back, shards of glass flying and tinkling across the walkway. Jason stood half-crouched in the opening, as if in pain, clutching his pistol in front of him. "Freeze, scumbag. Police."

Sean swore, then raised his gun hand in the air, pointing his pistol at the sky. "You got me, copper."

"Throw the gun down away from you," Jason ordered.

"Whatever you say." Sean looked at Emma, his feral smile never wavering.

She tensed, keeping as still as possible so she didn't distract Jason.

Sean tossed the gun onto the gravel.

"On your knees," Jason ordered. "Hands out to your sides."

"Don't shoot, Officer." Sean chuckled, then low-

ered himself down onto one knee. He watched Emma
the whole time, still smiling. Then he winked.

She sucked in a sharp breath.

Sean whirled around, another pistol seemingly
magically appearing in his other hand. He squeezed
off two shots before Jason could even squeeze off
one. Jason collapsed forward onto the wooden deck.

"No, please, no." The words came out a raspy
whisper as Emma stared in horror at Jason's crumpled body.

Sean laughed and kicked his gun away. "Why
bring one gun to a gunfight when you can bring two,
I always say. Now, let's make sure you don't get up
this time, shall we?" He raised his gun, ready to deliver a kill shot, if Jason wasn't dead already.

Emma slammed her hand down on the horn.

Sean whirled around, swinging his pistol toward
her.

She dived toward the floorboard. But instead of
hearing more gunshots, she heard something else.

A siren.

Had the cashier called 911 after all?

The sound of a vehicle's tires crunching on gravel
had Sean swearing.

Emma lay there frozen, afraid to move in case he
was waiting to shoot at her.

The next sounds she heard were boots running
across the wooden planks and a vehicle sliding across
the gravel into the parking lot, siren blaring.

She edged up out of the floorboard, ready to duck down again if she saw Sean.

The truck door flew open and the bore of a pistol was suddenly pointing at her.

She bit her lip so hard, the metallic taste of blood filled her mouth.

The pistol jerked up and away. "Emma, what the hell?"

She blinked. "Macon? Thank God, Macon." She scrambled out of the floorboard and plopped onto the bench seat. "Careful, he's in the store. Or maybe hiding around the left side of the building. He's got a gun." She whipped back toward the windshield. "Jason." She pointed, her throat so tight she could barely force the words out. "He shot Jason, two different times. By the truck, and in front of the store."

His jaw tightened as he looked toward the store. "Sean Hopper?"

"Yes. He must have followed us here. But I never saw a vehicle. I think he may have parked behind the building, maybe in an employee parking lot." She glanced past him. "Are you alone? No backup?"

He stood with his pistol pointed at the store as he scanned the building and nearby trees. "Backup's on the way. Jason had texted me this address earlier and I was already headed here to check on you when the call came in. I was worried it would be a good place for an ambush."

"I'm so sorry," Emma whispered. "I should have thought of that."

"No, Jason should have thought of that. And he should have told you to let me pick up your supplies instead of letting you come out here. Is anyone else inside the store?"

"It's not Jason's fault, I—"

"Is anyone else in the store?"

"Sorry. The cashier, I assume. He disappeared when the shots started. He must be hiding. I don't think Sean did anything to him but I'm not sure."

"Get back down in the floorboard. The engine block should stop any bullets if he shoots this way."

He radioed dispatch through his police transmitter, giving a quick update and telling them *officer down*. "Emma, backup will be here soon. They're just a few minutes out. I hate to leave you, but I have to check on Jason."

"Go. Help him."

"Wait here. Do not get out of the truck." He motioned behind him. "Bogart. Up."

Bogie hopped into the truck, forcing Emma to scrunch down into the floorboard again.

Macon issued a command in German. Bogie's demeanor changed instantly. Ears pricked forward, hackles raised. He stared through the windshield, alert for any sign of danger.

Macon shut the door.

"Wait," Emma called out. "You need Bogie more than me. Take him with you."

Her only answer was the sound of crunching gravel as he took off running.

Chapter Twenty-Two

Macon trained his gun toward the store as he crouched beside Jason. He risked a quick glance down, but didn't see any blood. A quick pat against Jason's chest sent a wave of relief through Macon. Jason was wearing his Kevlar vest. But that didn't mean a bullet hadn't entered through an armhole and hit something vital. It was rare, but it happened.

Continuing to scan the side of the building and store beyond, alert for any signs of movement, he ran his hand up Jason's vest to his neck where he pressed against the carotid artery, feeling for a pulse.

"Aren't you supposed to buy me dinner before getting this fresh?" Jason's voice wheezed out of him.

Macon couldn't help laughing. "Son of a... I thought you were dead."

"I *feel* dead." He coughed. "Hard...to breathe. Jerk hit me at least..." He gasped, obviously struggling. "Four...times."

"Probably broke a rib, punctured a lung. Help is on the way. Stop blabbing and save your air."

"Stop…being…so bossy."

Macon risked another quick glance down. "Cal's going to be ticked if he has to train another recruit to replace you."

"Gee, excuse me…f…for incon…veniencing him."

"Danged straight. Better not die so you can pull your fair share around the station." He smiled to make sure Jason knew he was teasing.

Jason tried to smile back, but winced in pain. "I'll… think about it. Phone broken. Tried radio. Broken… too."

"Cal and the others will be here any minute. An ambulance is right behind them. Your initial radio call went through. Dispatch heard you, heard the gunshots."

"Did something…right…then. Didn't…leave… Ms. Daniels."

Macon squeezed Jason's hand. "You did fine before, too. I was too hard on you."

"Don't…p…patron…"

"Don't patronize you?"

Jason nodded.

"I'm not. You've done a fine job, Jason. Just hold on a few more minutes. That's what I need you to do now."

Macon hesitated. They were both sitting ducks if Sean came back. He looked toward the truck, saw Bogie still on alert. No one was anywhere near the truck. He scanned the trees again, then shoved his pistol into his holster. "This is gonna hurt like hell."

"What?" Jason cried out as Macon grabbed his vest and pulled him into the store.

He yanked him behind shelves that would hide them from view from the back door, then checked his pulse again. Thready, but even. He'd passed out from the pain but was still breathing. Barely. Keeping an eye out for Sean, he punched the police radio button on his shoulder.

"Officer down. Repeat, officer down. Possible collapsed lung, broken ribs and who knows what else. Where's that bus I called for?"

"The ambulance should be there any minute," Jenny assured him.

Macon gave her more details as he watched the truck outside, ready to take off running toward Emma if Sean came anywhere near it. As soon as he clicked off the radio, the welcome sound of sirens came from down the road out front.

A gunshot sounded outside. The bullet pinged off the metal shelving a few feet away. Macon swore and took a quick look past the end of the aisle. Sean was standing by a stack of feed visible through the now-propped-open back door, pointing his gun toward Macon.

Macon squeezed off a couple of shots, making Sean duck down.

Sean jumped out from the side of the feed bags, firing off several more rounds.

Macon dived to the side, coming up in a crouch by the counter, firing again.

A cruiser skidded across the gravel out front as it sharply turned into the parking lot. Macon jerked back toward the exit just in time to see Sean running for the trees.

Macon ran out the front door as Margaret Avery hopped out of her car. Just Macon's luck that one of the few officers without a K-9 was the first one to arrive. He could have really used a K-9 right now.

He motioned for Margaret to run to him as he headed back into the store.

She sprinted inside, skidding across the tile floor. Her eyes widened when she saw Jason.

"He's alive," Macon told her. "I think he has a punctured lung. Tell the EMTs that when they get here. Guard him, and Emma. She's in the truck outside with Bogie."

He drew his pistol, checked the magazine.

"What are you going to do?" she demanded.

"I'm going to finish this."

"No, Macon. Not by yourself. And I can't back you up if I'm guarding Jason and Emma."

"Then let's hope I don't need backup." He took off running through the back door.

He didn't bother checking the maze of feed bags stacked in the loading area. He'd seen a flash of white just inside the tree line as he'd spoken to Margaret. Sean was in those woods, trying to get away. That wasn't going to happen. Emma had suffered enough. And Macon didn't want to risk letting Sean get comfortable out there in the trees where he could start shooting at the officers as they arrived. Macon had to stop him before someone else got hurt, or killed.

More sirens sounded down the road, reassuring him that help would be here in a matter of seconds. Knowing it was a huge risk, he took off running again, zigzagging toward the trees in an evasive maneuver.

A shot rang out, barely missing him as he zagged to the right.

Macon fired toward where he'd seen the gun flash in the dark woods.

More shots rang out. Macon swore and fired repeatedly toward the trees.

Engines roared out front. Tires spun on gravel. Sirens shattered the serenity of the forest.

Macon zigged left again. But his boot slipped on some loose rocks, knocking him off-balance. He fell to the ground just as Sean Hopper dived out from behind a huge oak tree, leveling his pistol at Macon.

A dark blur ran past Macon as he twisted around, trying to get his gun aimed at Sean before Sean shot him.

Sean screamed and fell back beneath a hundred pounds of snarling teeth and black fur. Bogie.

Macon frowned. Bogie was supposed to be protecting Emma. He turned around. Emma stood at the corner of the building, watching him. She'd left the safety of the truck and had ordered Bogie to protect him. Fury swept through Macon.

"Get him off me! Get him off me. He's killing

me!" Sean screamed and thrashed on the ground as Bogie sank his teeth into his arm.

Cal and Dillon both sprinted to Macon, pistols drawn and pointing at Sean.

Macon slowly holstered his pistol, his chest heaving from exertion.

"Help me!" Sean cried.

Cal arched a brow at Macon. "You gonna call him off or let him keep playing with his new chew toy."

Macon yelled an order in German. Bogie immediately let Sean go and backed away. But he didn't go far. He stood guard, hackles raised, teeth bared, as Cal moved in to handcuff Sean.

Macon didn't wait around. Instead, he motioned for Dillon to come with him back to the building. They stopped in front of Emma.

Her eyes were wide as she stared up at him. "Macon, thank God you're okay."

He leaned toward her, so angry he was shaking. "You were supposed to wait in the truck, with Bogie. You could have been killed."

She blinked in surprise. "But Sean was shooting at you. There wasn't any backup. You needed help."

"I needed you to be safe," he gritted out. He motioned to Dillon. "Get her out of here."

Macon headed into the store to check on Jason. But not before he caught the hurt look Emma aimed at him as Dillon led her away.

Chapter Twenty-Three

Emma curled her legs under her on the couch as Chief Walters sat beside her, droning on about everything that had happened in the past few days since the shoot-out at Sampson's Feed and Grain.

"Sean knows the DNA will come back proving he was here," Walters continued. "And of course, there's no way of getting out of what happened at the store. Too many witnesses, not to mention the security cameras. He's trying to make a deal with the prosecutor. But he doesn't have anything to bargain with. He'll do hard time, might even get life when you take into account attempted murder of two different police officers."

She tried to smile. "Sounds good. He won't be out to hurt Celia anymore. Or Anna. And you said Jason's doing well?"

Walters laughed. "He was, until Tashya walked in on him flirting with one of the nurses. It was all in fun. I know he didn't mean anything by it. And the doctor said he was half out of it because of the pain meds and probably didn't realize what he was doing. But he'll have to grovel for a long time before Tashya forgives him."

"I'm sure she will, though. It's obvious how much they care about each other. Jason was always anxious to go home to her after his shifts were over here at DCA."

"I'm sure she will. What about you? Are you going to forgive Macon?"

She blinked. "Excuse me?"

He sighed and took one of her hands in his. "Emma, you know I love you like you're my very own daughter. And I understand all the pain and trauma you've been through in your life, probably better than anyone else. But you continue trying to ignore and avoid love to keep from getting hurt. You and Macon are meant for each other. And you need to forgive him and move past how he treated you at the store after the shoot-out."

She tugged her hand from his. "What is with everyone trying to dissect my feelings and act like they know what's best for me? Besides, you have it all wrong. There's nothing for me to forgive. Macon was right. Logically. And I understand how he feels and why he was so angry with me. But at the same time, even if I could go back and change what I did, I wouldn't. Because Macon could have been killed. There's no way past that."

His brow furrowed. "Have you even spoken to him since that day?"

She crossed her arms. "Was there anything else you wanted to tell me about the investigation?"

He sighed again, his eyes sad. "Just that your pickup is still in evidence. The wheels of justice move slowly, even when a suspect is going to plead guilty. It might be a few weeks before I can get it released."

"It's okay. Barbara has offered to take me anywhere I need to go. And Piper picked up the dog food we needed in order to get us by until another feed store makes a delivery."

"Good, good. Where is Barbara? I thought she'd be here with Anna."

"Now that we're no longer under lock and key, she's taken Anna to a park in town. And after that, she's keeping her at her place overnight. She said I've been hogging Anna and it's her turn to play mommy for a few days." Emma smiled. "She also said it was high time she let Anna gum a French fry and get a taste of Idaho heaven."

"Fry sauce?"

"Of course."

They both laughed.

The chief leaned over and pressed a kiss against Emma's forehead. "I love you, sweet daughter. You take care of yourself, all right?"

She reached out and hugged him tightly against her. "I love you too. Dad."

When they pulled back, his eyes were suspiciously bright.

Once he'd left, Emma stood at the back door,

looking up at the mountains. They were already wearing little caps of snow in the higher elevations. Winter would be here before long. It was so peaceful looking at the beauty of nature, and she was so lucky to have a little piece of Idaho all to herself. But she was beginning to realize something else. After the aggravation of having someone in the house with her 24/7 for so long, the quiet and solitude she'd longed for wasn't what she'd hoped it would be. Instead of feeling restful and relieved, she felt…lonely.

She missed Macon.

She missed him so much she couldn't sleep at night. She couldn't eat. She was a bundle of nervous energy most of the time, feeling anxious, as if she was going to jump out of her own skin. Loving him and losing him was even worse than she'd dreaded it could be. And they'd never even really dated, or kissed aside from that one time. How much worse would she feel right now if she had allowed herself to get closer to him? If she'd given herself completely, body and soul? All this time she'd tried to guard her heart so she wouldn't feel this way. But she hadn't been able to guard it and had fallen in love. Now that she'd lost her chance with Macon, she'd learned something she'd never expected to learn.

He was worth the pain.

That cliché really was true, about loving and losing or never loving at all. She was in love with Macon. No question. And even though he was out of her life now, and she'd probably never see him again, she was glad that she'd shared those touches of his hand, basked in his sweet, gentle smile, felt the heat of that amazing kiss. Her one small glimpse into what it might have been like to have a life with him was more than some people had their entire lifetime. She was so blessed to have experienced even a small taste of how it could have been.

She stood at the back door a long time, feeling the pain, thinking about the conclusions she'd drawn. The sun was sinking behind the mountains now, casting long shadows across the deck. Good grief, she'd been here for at least an hour, thinking, mulling things over. And she'd come to a new conclusion.

"What a load of crock."

She didn't want to cherish the time she'd had with Macon and wallow in memories for the rest of her life. She'd been wallowing in memories ever since her little sister and brother were killed. It was time to actually *live*. She wanted more.

She wanted Macon.

And if that meant groveling and begging him to forgive her, that's what she'd do. But she wasn't giving up without a fight. She loved him. Truly, deeply, irrevocably. And for the first time ever, she was going to fight for love instead of being afraid of it.

She headed into the family room and grabbed her phone off the end table. Drawing a deep breath, she punched his number.

He answered on the first ring.

"Emma, hi. I was just about to—"

"Don't hang up on me, Macon."

"I wasn't going to—"

"We need to talk."

"Okay."

"Face-to-face."

"I agree. That's why I—"

"I mean it. No more avoiding the elephant in the room. I wouldn't change what I did at the feed store even if I could. And I understand why that makes you angry. Because you care about me."

"Yes. I do."

"O-okay." She swallowed. "And you were worried about me."

"Yes. I was."

"But I was worried about you, too. I couldn't have lived with myself if I didn't send Bogie in there to help you and you got hurt, or worse. Can you understand that?"

"I understand. Emma, I—"

"No. Don't stop me. I have to say this before I lose my nerve. I love you, Macon. Do you hear me? I. Love. You. I love you so much it hurts. I'm sorry that I hurt you, at the station. I was scared and—"

"I know. The chief explained a lot to me, about the trauma you've gone through. How scared it made you to let someone past that wall you built around your heart."

"He…he did? You understand?"

"I do."

She swallowed. "Can you forgive me? For every-thing?"

"I thought we weren't supposed to apologize?"

"I'm invoking the jerk clause. I was a jerk. I need you to forgive me."

"You've never been a jerk. If you need me to say I forgive you, then okay. I forgive you. But only if you forgive me, too."

She clutched the phone so hard her hand hurt. "There's nothing to forgive."

"Emma—"

"Okay. Okay. Yes. I forgive you. And I love you."

"Emma. I think we should be having this conver-sation face-to-face. Don't you?"

"Yes. Of course. I just wasn't sure you'd even talk to me so I—"

"Emma."

"Yes, Macon."

"Open the front door."

She blinked, then slowly crossed to the door. She pulled it open, still holding the phone to her ear.

Macon stood there, his phone to his ear, too. And the look of love in his eyes as he stared down at her stole her breath.

"I love you, Emma," he spoke into the phone.

"I love you, too." She threw her phone down, cry-ing tears of joy as she jumped into his arms.

Epilogue

"We pulled it off." Emma leaned against Macon's side, reveling in the feel of his arm around her waist as they watched the chaos taking place inside the training ring.

"We sure did. I think almost everyone in the police department is here, with their families. Even your orange cat, Gus, made an appearance. I saw him stealing a corn dog off someone's plate earlier."

She laughed. "It won't be his last today."

"Probably not. Best Daniels Canine Academy anniversary celebration ever. Or so I've been told."

She smiled. "It will be hard to top it next year. I pulled outstanding dog trainers and K-9s from all over Idaho to put on this performance. And I hired the best caterers I could find to make all that delicious finger food in the tents."

"Not to mention your homemade fry sauce. It's amazing."

"It is, isn't it?"

"I would never lie about something as sacred as fry sauce."

She laughed, looking around, enjoying the sheer joy on everyone's faces as they played games, watched the exhibitions and ate an obscene amount of food. "I understand Rutledge not being here since he doesn't support the K-9 program. But it's still kind of sad since he's the second-in-command. Seems like he should be here with everyone else."

He gently turned her around to face him. "You haven't heard the news?"

"News?"

"Rutledge resigned."

She stared at him in shock. "What? Why? I thought he was looking forward to being the new chief."

"He was. Until Chief Walters told him he's moving up his retirement to this Friday. And that the new chief will be Cal Hoover. Rutledge resigned on the spot and walked out."

She pressed a hand to her throat. "Oh, my. That's… unexpected."

"It was a long time coming. Just in the short time that I've been here, I've seen that the rumors are true. In spite of how smart and gifted Rutledge is with police work, his people skills are lacking. He doesn't treat others with the respect they deserve even with the extensive coaching Walters gave him. It would have been a disaster for morale if he'd become chief. But if you're worried about his future, don't be. He's too talented not to land on his feet with some other police force. Hopefully he'll have learned a lesson from what happened here and will treat people better wherever he goes."

"Maybe. I hope so. Wow, this Friday, huh? I didn't realize the chief was going to retire so soon. I thought he was going to wait another year or so."

"Apparently he wanted to make it coincide closely with your anniversary party. I imagine he'll give a speech to officially announce it soon." He leaned down close to her ear. "And then he'll let everyone know that Theresa is retiring, too, and they're both going to move in together."

She jerked back to look him in the eyes. "Serious?"

"Serious. He told me this morning."

She lightly punched his chest. "How did you get so plugged into the grapevine? He never shared any of that with me."

"Maybe he wanted to surprise you. Or maybe he didn't go into all of that yet because you've been so busy helping Celia and little Anna." He pointed and she turned around.

Celia was sitting with Anna at the face-painting booth. Little Anna was squealing with delight, watching the other children. She was too young to hold still long enough to have her own face done. But she kept bouncing on Celia's knee and clapping her hands together in her excitement.

Emma wiped her eyes and sniffed.

"Are you crying?" Macon leaned down to look at her. "You are. Why?"

"They're happy tears. I love both of them so much. And I'm so happy that Celia has earned back custody of Anna. She's worked so hard to get to that point. I'm also relieved she won't have to worry about Sean any more. He'll be an old man by the time he gets out of prison, no threat to either of them."

He gently feathered her hair back from her face. "I know you miss having Anna around all the time."

She smiled up at him. "I miss her, yes. But my husband makes me happy every day." She moved her hand to her stomach, which was still flat, but soon wouldn't be. "And his love and patience convinced me that I could be a good mom, in spite of my fears."

"You'll be the best. I've zero doubts." He gently kissed her before straightening.

She stared up at him, her heart full. "If it's a boy, I was thinking a nice name might be Ken."

His eyes widened and his arms tightened around her. "Are you sure?"

"Of course. I know how much your partner meant to you, how much he still means to you. You've worked so hard to get past the grief and survivor's guilt. I don't want to do anything to make it worse again. If you think it would be too difficult—"

"No." He cleared his throat, then smiled. "No, it's getting easier every day, partly because of the therapy you insisted on, but mainly because of you. Ken, and his family, would be honored if we name our baby after him. And if it's a girl, maybe we could name her Susan, after your mom."

Her eyes turned misty. "I'd like that, very much. Thank you, Macon."

He pressed a whisper-soft kiss against her lips. "Thank you, sweet Emma."

In reply, she pulled him down for a longer, deeper kiss that had him groaning with regret when it ended.

"When is this dang party going to be over?" he complained. "We need some serious alone time."

She laughed, so happy her heart felt as if it would burst from joy. Macon was the love of her life, and they were building a family together. But it had taken the tragedy of nearly losing him for her to realize that love was worth fighting for. And that families came in all different forms. She'd thought she'd lost her family when she was a little girl. But the moment that Rick and Susan Daniels had opened their home and hearts to her, she'd gained a new family. Then she'd lost them too and thought that was it for her. Macon had shown her that wasn't true, and that all she had to do was look around right now to see just how huge her family had become.

Macon, Anna, Celia, everyone in Jasper PD— they were her family. It didn't matter that they weren't blood related. Their bond was stronger than genetics. Because they chose each other, chose to be there every day, no matter what. Just as she and Macon had chosen each other.

"Ready?" He held his hand out toward her.

She laced her fingers through his. "Ready. Take me to our family, Macon."

He smiled and led her across the field.

* * * * *

*Don't miss the previous books in the
K-9s on Patrol series:*

Decoy Training *by Caridad Piñeiro*
Sniffing Out Danger *by Elizabeth Heiter*
Foothills Field Search *by Maggie Wells*
Alpha Tracker *by Cindi Myers*
Scent Detection *by Leslie Marshman*

*Available now wherever
Harlequin Intrigue books are sold!*

WE HOPE YOU ENJOYED
THIS BOOK FROM

⊕HARLEQUIN

INTRIGUE

Seek thrills. Solve crimes. Justice served.

Dive into action-packed stories that will keep you
on the edge of your seat. Solve the crime
and deliver justice at all costs.

6 NEW BOOKS AVAILABLE EVERY MONTH!

The whole desperate plan began simply as a last-ditch attempt to save his life. He never intended for anyone to get hurt. That day, not long after Thanksgiving, he walked into the bank full of hope. It was the first time he'd ever asked for a loan. It was also the first time he'd ever seen executive loan officer Carla Richmond.

When he tapped at her open doorway, she looked up from that big desk of hers. He thought she was too young and pretty with her big blue eyes and all that curly chestnut-brown hair to make the decision as to whether he lived or died.

She had a great smile as she got to her feet to offer him a seat.

He felt so out of place in her plush office that he stood in the doorway nervously kneading the brim of his worn baseball cap for a moment before stepping in. As he did, her blue-eyed gaze took in his ill-fitting clothing hanging on his rangy body, his bad haircut, his large, weathered hands.

He told himself that she'd already made up her mind before he even sat down. She didn't give men like him a second look—let alone money. Like his father always said, bankers never gave dough to poor people who actually needed it. They just helped their rich friends.

Right away Carla Richmond made him feel small with her questions about his employment record, what he had for collateral, why he needed the money and how he planned to repay it. He'd recently lost one crappy job and was in the process of starting another temporary one, and all he had to show for the years he'd worked hard labor since high school was an old pickup and a pile of bills.

He took the forms she handed him and thanked her, knowing he wasn't going to bother filling them in. On the way out of her office, he balled them up and dropped them in the trash. All the way to his pickup, he mentally kicked himself for being such a fool. What had he expected?

No one was going to give him money, even to save his life—especially some woman in a suit behind a big desk in an air-conditioned office. It didn't matter that she didn't have a clue how desperate he really was. All she'd seen when she'd looked at him was a loser. To think that he'd bought a new pair of jeans with the last of his cash and borrowed a too-large button-up shirt from a former coworker for this meeting.

After climbing into his truck, he sat for a moment, too scared and sick at heart to start the engine. The worst part was the thought of going home and telling Jesse. The way his luck was going, she would walk out on him. Not that he could blame her, since his gambling had gotten them into this mess.

He thought about blowing off work, since his new job was only temporary anyway, and going straight to the bar. Then he reminded himself that he'd spent the last of his money on the jeans. He couldn't even afford a beer. His own fault, he reminded himself. He'd only made things worse when he'd gone to a loan shark for cash and then stupidly gambled the money, thinking he could make back what he owed and then some when he won. He'd been so sure his luck had changed for the better when he'd met Jesse.

Last time the two thugs had come to collect the interest on the loan, they'd left him bleeding in the dirt outside his rented house. They would be back any day.

With a curse, he started the pickup. A cloud of exhaust blew out the back as he headed home to face Jesse with the bad news. Asking for a loan had been a long shot, but still he couldn't help thinking about the disappointment he'd see in her eyes when he told her. They'd planned to go out tonight for an expensive dinner with the loan money to celebrate.

As he drove home, his humiliation began to fester like a sore that just wouldn't heal. Had he known even then how this was going to end? Or was he still telling himself he was just a nice guy who'd made some mistakes, had some bad luck and gotten involved with the wrong people?

Don't miss
Christmas Ransom *by B.J. Daniels,*
available December 2022 wherever
Harlequin books and ebooks are sold.

Harlequin.com

HARLEQUIN
PLUS

Announcing a **BRAND-NEW** multimedia subscription service for romance fans like you!

Read, Watch and Play.

Experience the easiest way to get the romance content you crave.

Start your **FREE 7 DAY TRIAL** at
www.harlequinplus.com/freetrial.